Hunkered Down

Hunkered Down
By

Sterling Rogers

JoNa Books
Bedford, Indiana

ISBN: 0-9657929-4-3

Library of Congress Number: 00 131107

1st Printing January 2001

INDEX

PREFACE

We were not extraordinary men, neither the captives nor our captors. We represented neither the best nor the worst of our respective cultures. Among us there was no Saint Francis of Assisi nor Attila the Hun, none of the heroic rhetoric of a Churchill nor the mad rantings of a Hitler. We were men caught in circumstances not of our own making, circumstances whose root causes we understood only imperfectly if, indeed, we understood them at all.

We were prisoners of the German *Kriegsgefangenenlager* system and the guards appointed to insure that the system operated. We were, for the most part, boys and old men with very rarely one of mature years in between. Most of the prisoners were boys still, in their teens and very early twenties. Most of the guards were men too old to qualify for combat duty, sometimes handicapped by physical disabilities as well. Together we constituted a world apart, but a world existing within the structure of wartime Germany.

This, then, is the story of that world told not as history but as a montage of memory. I have made no effort to research the events related so as to insure their accuracy of time and personalities involved. I have not tried to record specifics. On the contrary, I have taken incidents and characters as I remember them or as others have told about them, and have tried to bring their story alive.

I have not intended a dramatic story. These are little tales told because they seemed worth telling. If they have a central theme at all, and I am not sure they do, it is the very human-ness of humanity.

The Crew

Photo was made before we had a co-pilot assigned. The airplane was just a convenient backdrop. Left to right, front: Earl Osborn, Robert Masten, Oral Moore, Henry Dunning, Tom Fairchild, John Frangedakis. Top: Len Sexton, Livingstone Hearne, Sterling Rogers. No photos are available of Gene Koury, co-pilot, and Robert Pelletier, navigator, who were on our last mission. Hearne did not fly that mission.

Hunkered Down

Settling In

The notice on the cook shack bulletin board read:

"Block meeting tonight

Block 157

After *Appell*"

No details were given, just the bare facts -- the implied command to be present in the barracks immediately after the evening *appell* formation, the headcount of the prisoners. And it was signed by the senior officer in the compound. I was not yet able to negotiate the distance to the cook house so the others brought the news back to me.

But it was repeated again and again and speculated on by everyone. There was no doubt that something important was being planned but it had to be something approved of by the Germans, else the notice would not have been posted openly.

Through the long afternoon we wondered about it and, periodically, someone would be sent again to the bulletin board to see if anything had been added to the notice. But it was always the same. No one thought of doing the obvious thing, asking the colonel or one of his staff what was planned. We waited and wondered.

When the others finally were called out to the rain-soaked field for the headcount formation I stumped about in the room, unable to settle down, yet unable to move freely either because of the clumsy cast on my leg. Without crutches I was a human grasshopper, going noisily from my bunk to the stove to the window and back again to my bunk.

A guard popped his head in the door, glanced at the slip of paper which authorized me to remain in the barracks, grunted something in German and then went away. I moved again to sit by the window where I could see the first movement when the others began to return. Somehow, I was always uncomfortable waiting alone in a room.

They came back, stamping and scraping the mud from their boots before entering the hallway. We were all new to the business of being prisoners and eager to learn what the meeting was about. So we crowded together in the hallway and waited for the arrival of the colonel. Someone brought me a stool and put it down in the front of the others so that I would be able to see and hear without the strain of standing on one leg the whole time.

When the colonel finally came he was trailed by several other Americans and a German sergeant. The sergeant stood self-importantly at one side while the Americans arranged themselves in a sort of backdrop to the colonel. We shuffled our feet and waited expectantly.

There were the usual statements about being military men even though we were prisoners of war, about maintaining our pride and discipline, and then the colonel got down to the business of the meeting: he was appointing a block chief and an assistant who were old hands in the compound. They would move into the block the next day and would be responsible for guiding us, the new prisoners, in adjusting to life in the POW camps. They were Bud and George, men whom most of us knew slightly from having seen them around the area. They each said a few words and then the colonel left. When he was gone, with the German sergeant scurrying behind so as not to be left, Bud called again for attention and introduced to us a man who had become a sort of living legend in the camps of Silesia, a man who could tell us more about survival than anyone else. Although we were new arrivals we had heard about Tex and his activities. In other compounds he had organized entertainment by the prisoners for the prisoners, he had got up a fairly good band in spite of the lack of sheet music, and he had started a camp newspaper. There were whispered stories about escapes he had helped to plan and the ingenious ways he had found to carry them out. Everyone knew that he was one of the survivors of the tunnel attempt of the previous year and that alone was enough to make him an "elder statesman" of the camp. And through it all Tex stood as a monolith of calm and confidence. He spoke at some length about the necessity for keeping one's mind occupied, of self-discipline, of tolerance for others, and he ended his talk with a sort of parable that struck home with me and, I suspect, with most of the others.

"I'm a country boy," he said, rocking back on his heels as if he still wore the boots that were as much a part of his upbringing as the drawl that he used when he said it. "And where I come from we have to know and understand the ways of our livestock if we are to survive. When a norther blows in and the snow is flyin' level with the ground a cow will drift with it. She'll keep driftin' till she hits a fence. And then she'll stand and freeze to death if nobody comes to get her movin' again.

"But a horse is different. When a blizzard comes he'll find a chaparral bush to break the wind and he'll hunker down and wait it out. And that's what you will have to do. Find something to occupy your mind and hunker down. This war can't go on forever."

And that is just what we did. For the next year we hunkered down and waited.

II

Terrorfliegers

The First Mission

In the plexiglass nose of the B-17 there was a small round window. It was closed with a stout metal latch. I don't remember what the original purpose of it was, but our only use for it was ventilation while on the ground. As we taxied out for take-off I found the latch had been broken and the window would not stay closed. The navigator took a couple of flak vests and shoved them against the window. "There. That will keep it shut," he said. Neither of us wanted to be the cause of an aborted mission. We didn't tell the pilot about it.

As we got airborne the flak vests began to give way to the stream of air forcing its way inside. I put my right foot against them to keep them in place. It was not a comfortable position and I did not relish the thought that I would have to maintain it for hours, but it was preferable to being the cause of an abort.

Our take-off and assembly were uneventful. It could have been a practice mission back in the States. The climb to altitude showed thickening clouds over the European continent, but we had known it would be partly cloud-covered. Six tenths cloud cover meant we would have forty percent clear air. That was enough to get a good sighting on the target before the bombs dropped. It should be easy.

New crews assigned to combat units were not expected to go into action without some guidance from experienced personnel. At least not the officers on the crew. The bombardier, the navigator, and the two pilots were assigned individually to fly their first mission with other crews who had seen action a number of times. It was a good policy. It meant your first combat flight was with strangers, but they were men who had been there before. They knew what to expect. It was a scary time, but knowing that they had done this before made it a little less so.

I flew my first mission with a crew who were finishing their tour and getting ready to go home. My state of nerves was not helped by the navigator's comment that he hoped I was not a bad-luck charm - that he really wanted this last mission to be a milk-run.

I did too. The early morning briefing, however, indicated it was not going to be so. Our target was Nancy. The weather prediction was for six tenths cloud cover. That meant the lead bombardier would have a limited time to get his sight synchronized and bombs dropped. The target of second choice was Metz and, again, the same cloud cover was predicted. Both targets were heavily defended by anti-aircraft guns. Some fighter opposition could also be expected.

We would be flying with minimum escort. Most of the escort force was being used to protect raids on interior Germany. Targets in France were usually less well defended by the *Luftwaffe*, but they were heavily defended by ack-ack guns. It was not going to be easy.

When we arrived at the plane I found that the bombsight had not been mounted on its autopilot base. It was brought out to me by the armorer, buttoned into its canvas carrying case. He assured me that the regular bombardier always wanted it that way. I was surprised and nervous about the whole situation. The bombsight was, at the time, one of our most closely-guarded secrets. It would normally be moved from vault to aircraft under armed guard and, when it was installed in the aircraft, a guard stood by until the bombardier took charge before the flight. This one was being carried around by an unarmed man. And it was being carried in a thin canvas case which showed all of its contours and shapes.

I was astonished but I took the sight and mounted it myself. I hurriedly cranked in the pre-determined data just in case I got a chance to use it. I didn't expect to, really. I was the new boy on the block and would certainly not be given the chance to lead the formation over the target. We would all drop our bomb loads on a signal from the lead bombardier. That was how it was done.

Over the North Sea, as we circled and waited for the entire wing to assemble, my right foot began to go numb from the constant pressure against the vent hatch and its two flak vests. I shifted my position so that I could get my left foot on it. That was some relief but it meant I was in an awkward position to use my guns and bomb sight.

We crossed the coast at Dunkirk, making a straight line for Nancy. There was no need to waste gasoline and flying time in an effort to fool the gunners on the ground. That part of occupied France was so filled with possible targets that subterfuge was a waste of time. And one target was no more valuable to the Germans than the next. They would defend the entire area, not some single target.

I shifted my position occasionally, trying to relieve the tension of keeping that vent hatch closed. We wore electrically heated suits and could have survived the cold, but we would have been miserable.

The briefing officer had said we could expect heavy ack-ack and possible fighter attacks. We saw neither. There was an eerie calm that left us holding our breath and looking anxiously into the distance. Even as we approached our target there was no opposition. As the entire wing swung onto the approach and the lead bombardier began his synchronization run, even then there was no opposition.

Below, between the scudding clouds, I could see the saw-tooth roofs of the target. I put the telescope of my sight on it to be sure it was the true target. Clouds flicked across the field of vision, but I could have dropped my bombs on the target. The crosshairs of my scope stayed fixed on the center of the complex of buildings as the clouds alternately hid them and then revealed them to me.

The order to drop never came. No bombs hit Nancy that day. The lead bombardier had been unable to synchronize his sight on the target. He was distracted by the scudding clouds and un-nerved by the eerie quiet of having no flak and no fighters. We turned toward Metz and our secondary target. No burst of flak, not a single fighter, nothing had been shown in the way of opposition.

It was only a matter of minutes to Metz and the cloud cover was the same. I made a quick check of my target information folder to be sure I could recognize the target and changed the preset data in my bombsight because of the different target and approach direction.

Again I could see the target through the broken clouds below. Again I checked my sight to be sure it would be synchronized if I should be called on to use it. And again the lead bombardier never gave the order to drop our bombs.

Two target chances gone. Now we were down to hitting a target of opportunity. Having failed to hit the two assigned targets, the lead bombardier was free to drop on any target he found convenient and vulnerable. I was frustrated and angry because I felt I could have hit either one, but I could do nothing about it.

Both my legs were numb from the strain of holding the vent hatch closed. And the lead crew seemed determined to take us home with full bomb loads. They headed straight back toward the base in East Anglia. I was beginning to worry about getting rid of the bombs over the North Sea rather than try a landing with the bomb bays loaded when the word was passed that we would hit the airfield at Ostend.

Ostend was known to be protected by some big guns. Lots of big guns. They put up a box barrage every time Allied planes crossed the area. There was obviously something down there the Germans didn't want us to damage. And this lead crew, who missed two good targets because of six tenths cloud cover, was going to lead us into that maelstrom of anti-aircraft fire. It didn't make sense. I could not change anything. We would follow our leader.

Long before we reached the target we could see the first tentative puffs of ack-ack. As we drew nearer they became more frequent until, over the city of Ostend there was a black box of smoke from fifteen thousand feet up. And we were going to fly into it.

We swung on course for the bomb run. The planes bucked and heaved as the pilots tried to hold them steady in spite of the anti-aircraft fire all around us. Frigid air rushed in around the flak vests as the heaving plane made me momentarily lose my balance. The lead bombardier was once again trying to get his sight synchronized on a target. The bombardiers of all the other ships opened their bomb bays when the lead ship did. The bombardiers sat, one hand on the toggle switch, the other holding an earphone against one ear, ready to drop the entire load of bombs on the signal from the lead ship.

Suddenly our ship lurched upward and to the left. The world seemed to be on fire. I was aware of a fireball outside our aluminum and plexiglass bubble. My first thought was that we had been hit, for the ship was bouncing and bucking uncontrollably.

"My God." The navigator's voice on the interphone carried a sense of prayer more than profanity. "He just blew up." The plane off our right wing was no longer there.

"Do you see any parachutes?" The captain was concerned about survivors even though he was having a hard time controlling his own plane.

"No chutes," the tail gunner reported. "Must have got a flak burst right in the bomb bay."

No one asked what crew it was. Everyone knew. Everyone lost a friend or two when that ship was blasted out of the air.

We did not know it at the time, but two other crews went down in that few seconds over Ostend. Nine chutes were seen coming from one plane, but none from the other. Three crews lost on a target of opportunity. Thirty men. Thirty friends.

And, in the final analysis, the whole mission was a failure. We not only lost three crews and three aircraft, we put our bombs into the sea. The lead bombardier was so nervous that he over-shot the target and all our bombs landed in the shallow water off shore from the airfield.

I told myself I could have hit any one of the three targets. But could I, really? I probably would have been just as nervous as our lead man was, and I might have done even worse than he did. He didn't have to keep one foot firmly in place against the vent hatch.

Mulheim?

East Anglia in April can be glorious. It isn't always so, but in 1944 the last few days of the month were perfect. Stewey and I took advantage of what little time off we got to wander through the local countryside. It is Constable country. Each farm house, each country church, looked as if it came directly from a Constable painting

But we were left little time to enjoy the scenery. Most days we were wakened at four in the morning, to be fed breakfast, briefed, and sent out on a mission. Sometimes it was real and sometimes it was only practice. But it kept us so busy we had no time to regret lost leisure.

On one of those mornings when the faint light of dawn was just beginning to outline the hangars against the eastern sky, the briefing officer pulled the curtain from the mission map to reveal a bright red line pointing into the heart of the Rhineland. I don't remember the target name. It wasn't Essen nor Koln nor Dusseldorf. It might have been Mulheim. I just don't remember.

Whatever the target, it was obvious this was not going to be a milk run. The industrial towns along the Rhine were heavily defended. In large part the German war effort depended on them for production. If Hitler lost the Rhineland he had pretty much lost the war.

We took off that morning into clear skies. As we raced down the runway to lift-off little swirling ribbons of condensation trailed from our wing tips. The runway surface was wet from the heavy dew but the air was clear and heady with the scents of spring.

Contrails formed behind us as we climbed to altitude and circled over the North Sea, waiting for the entire group to assemble before we started east. Contrails made us conspicuous to gunners on the ground, but there was nothing anyone could do about them. They made us nervous, but their value to the enemy was negligible.

We picked up a fighter escort as we crossed the Dutch coast. Most of the opposition over Holland would probably come from the flak barges on the Zuider Zee, but there was always the chance the *Luftwaffe* would try to put up some of its fighter force in spite of a severe shortage of gasoline. The decision makers saw no reason to take chances, thus the escort.

The flak gunners did their best, but most of their shots burst far below us. All the way from the coast to the target one battery after another tried to reach us, to bring us down, to stop the inevitable bomb-drop. But our flight path kept us far above the reach of their guns. Seeing those black puffs was unnerving, but it is the one you don't see that does you in.

We hit our target with impunity. Not a plane nor a man had been lost. In the clear air the lead bombardier had put our bombs dead on the target. The pattern of explosions on the ground showed we had obliterated everything around the target center. It was an unqualified success.

But our escort had gone home. Fighter aircraft could not carry enough fuel to stay with the bombers for a full mission, and ours had to run for home while they could. If we met enemy fighters now we would be on our own. But the B-17 was not named Flying Fortress in vain. We carried 13 fifty caliber machine guns. We could surround ourselves with a wall of lead.

As we crossed the coast of Holland on our way home the tail gunner called on the intercom. "Hey, there's a Jug on our tail. And I think he's moving closer."

"Keep an eye on him. If he gets too close, warn him off with a shot across his bow." Somehow through all the training without a co-pilot or navigator, I had become the de facto second in command of the crew. At that moment the pilot had his hands full just flying the plane and keeping in formation, so it was my duty to make such decisions.

A second thought occurred to me. "Are you sure it is a Jug and not an FW-190?" The two aircraft looked very much alike when seen nose-on.

"No, it's a Jug. It's got American markings. But he keeps moving in." Johnny was getting very nervous about this stranger who was crowding his air space.

"Don't let him in. Make him stay outside gun range. Earl? Tom? Can you see him?"

"Yeah, I got 'im in my sights." It was the calm voice of Earl in the upper turret.

"OK. If he comes any closer fire enough in his direction to get a tracer or two. That should keep him at a distance." I really wasn't interested in being the one who shot down an American fighter plane, but I didn't want to be taken for a chump by some Kraut who had got his hands on enough paint to camouflage an FW, either.

The crew were silent for a minute or two, just keeping tabs on the fighter plane trailing us. Then Tom's voice came on again: "Hey, Tail End Charlie in the low echelon has spotted him too. I just saw the upper turret zero in on him."

"Well, keep him covered, just in case." I was worried about that lone fighter out there. It was not like an American fighter pilot to come into a bomber formation on his own. As long as he kept his nose toward us we really couldn't be sure he wasn't an FW wearing false colors. But I didn't want to alarm the crew if it wasn't necessary.

"He's moving in again." Johnny sounded panicky. I was afraid he would do something foolish, like fixating on the markings and not seeing the identifying details. He might be so convinced by the markings that he would fail to fire if the guy really made a pass at us.

"He's in my range now." Earl's calm voice had just a slight edge to it. "I'm not sure it's a Jug. Looks like the wrong airscoop shape to me."

"Don't give him a chance to fire. If he turns directly toward you, shoot him down." Earl's suspicions had meshed with mine and I was determined we would not be shot up by some imposter. If he was an American he should not be so close in.

"He's turning. He's coming in." Johnny was shouting into the microphone in his panic.

"Shoot the son-of-a-bitch down." I could not risk it any longer. Earl acted instantly. I could feel the shudder in the airframe as he let go with his upper turret. After a second's hesitation Johnny joined in. I knew he did because his microphone was open and I could hear the rattle of his guns.

It only lasted a few seconds. The fighter pulled away and started a rapid descent.

"I think you winged him. I saw oily smoke from his exhaust," Tom reported.

"Yeah, But he ain't no Jug," Earl said. "I got a good look at his silhouette as he pulled away. He's a 190 for sure."

We reported the incident at debriefing and it was confirmed by members of several other crews. Everyone had thought it was a P-47 at the time. Only Earl was convinced it was not. But a check of all the P-47's in the air that day showed no sign of a single straggler. So Johnny and Earl got credit for downing an FW-190.

Berlin

Our departure that morning was not particularly unusual. The crew navigator had a cold so we had been assigned a spare from another crew. Our briefings had gone well and we were full of the confidence and self-assurance of youth. Our plane had checked out with no obvious faults -- the bomb load, which was my special province, was loaded and safetied to my complete satisfaction.

Of course we experienced some misgivings -- at a time like this every man gives some thought to the fact that he may not survive. But our misgivings were only vaguely felt and totally unexpressed. We were much too busy with the details of readying ourselves and our equipment for the next six hours or so of flight. I recall going back a second time to check the safety wires on the bomb fuses because I had had the experience one time of having one work free, leaving a live bomb armed and ready to detonate in the bomb rack.

That business of the spare navigator did cause some minor concern because he was a stranger to us all, but he seemed so competent in checking out his guns that we dismissed our doubts quickly. After all, he had seen a lot more missions over Germany than the rest of us had -- one more after this one and he could go home.

So we climbed through the overcast and joined the swarm that was forming for the flight eastward. The early morning skies were streaked with the flares of lead ships calling their flights together -- two red and one green for us, the opposite for our sister outfit. We found our place almost immediately then circled endlessly with the rest of the formation while the stragglers labored through the cloud-deck and struggled upward into their assigned places. I used the time to get my bombsight set up with all of the previously calculated data. If I should be allowed to use it, those last-minute corrections would only take a few seconds and the time on the bomb run could be shortened accordingly.

If I should be allowed to use it. I carried a bombsight, but I was not the lead bombardier. Because we practiced pattern bombing it was standard procedure for all other bombardiers to toggle out their bombs on cue from the lead bombardier. This made for a highly destructive pattern of explosions on the target, but it also gave ulcers to bombardiers who had to sit through the interminable period of someone else's sight synchronization. What took me ten seconds to do seemed to take forever when someone else was doing it. Those sudden, fire-shot balls of smoke just beyond the plexiglass added urgency to the task. I could see them, but the lead bombardier could see only that little circle in his telescope.

If I should be allowed. But I didn't want that either because it would mean that the lead plane had gone down. We were flying the number two slot and so were prepared to take the lead if necessary, but we hoped it wouldn't be. Somehow you always set out with the idea that today would be a milk run and were a little surprised and upset when it didn't turn out that way.

After one final sweep above the Wash to gather the last straggling Fortresses into the formation we climbed eastward over the NorthSea. Our target was Berlin so we could not afford to make very many deviations from the direct route there. Besides, we counted on our numbers and our immense firepower to protect us more than on our evasiveness. Our altitude made anti-aircraft guns almost useless except for a barrage effect, and what fighter pilot in his right mind would face that imposing array of armament?

In mid-climb we picked up a mixed escort of 51s and Jugs. They idled along high above us like a pack of bird dogs, trotting first one way and then another, trying for the scent of the quarry. They seemed impatient with the idle pace, sometimes racing ahead and then turning to coax us on.

We expected flak from the coastal batteries and from the flak barges on the Zuider Zee and we were not disappointed. They did their best to lay a carpet of explosions but the deadly nap of it lay far below us. Those few explosions which reached our altitude burst so far ahead of us that it was obvious that the gunners had been misinformed in their expectations. They would correct their error before the second wave of planes came, but we were gone before they realized their loss.

We were gone deep into the heartland of Germany. We swept eastward majestically, a flying wedge aimed toward Berlin. Jerry was hard-pressed in those days to supply his fighter force with enough gasoline to defend against all of the attacks but we had expected more opposition than we had met so far. Intelligence had predicted continuous fighter attacks from the Zuider Zee on and, thus far, we had seen none. So we bored on, drawing a little closer together as we went, feeling a little distrustful of the inactivity and wondering when it would be shattered, as surely it must.

Air battles in movies are things of violent sound and motion, causing the focus of the eye and of the ear to blur with the force of it all. But that is not the way it really happens. The classic description of such things would have the Jerry burst upon us suddenly with a rattle of gunfire and a blast of action. Countless movies over the years have built these scenes to a crescendo of tenseness until it is sometimes difficult to remember that it wasn't that way at all.

We saw them first as tiny black dots far off to our right climbing toward our level; tiny, impersonal black dots that moved ever so slowly and silently upward. The escort inexplicably peeled off to the left and began to diminish into the distance. Then I saw that there were little black dots there, too. In every direction the little black dots were climbing and struggling upward, moving always in the same direction that we were; moving silently and menacingly. Moving to get ahead of and above the formation so that they could cut back through like a scythe. There was no sound save the drumming of the engines and the soft crackle of static in my earphones. The dots were there, moving ever so slowly upward and ahead of us, but they came no closer. We tracked them with our guns and fidgeted impatiently, but there was nothing more we could do. They were far out of range and pulling away.

Those next few minutes were an eternity that, strangely and in retrospect, seems to consist of vignettes and still shots and ghastly silence. I do not see in my mind's eye the swirls of motion and flashes of color that must necessarily compose such a battle. The ear of my memory retains no trace of the clatter and rattle of machine guns nor the drone of engines. Instead, I see the snout of a *Focke-Wolfe* suspended in perfect quarterings of the cross-hairs of a gunsight. I see the Fourth of July effect of an anti-aircraft shell exploding dead ahead -- not the violent motion of the explosion but the still photoplate of the outward thrust of thousands of bits of shrapnel. I feel again the jolting physical blows to the diaphragm when the ship was hit by explosions, that instant response by the human body to the overpowering resonance of TNT. A burst of flame is captured in my memory, but oddly not in color, as it streamed outward from an engine. Again a vignette, without any sense of motion, the flame and cowl flap in sharp focus, rapidly diffusing into a background of nothingness. There is the view of an engine oddly canted on its mounts in that instant before it dropped clear of the wing. The feel through my gloves of the bomb-bay switches and the sudden lift of the plane as the bombs fell away. The little hole in the bulkhead behind me still stands sharp in my mind, its tipsy L shape clearly seen in spite of the years. I did not know then, and years later I still do not know how that particular bit of shrapnel managed to travel from its point of origin in the explosion just beneath our bomb racks through the maze of cables and controls and bulkheads and instruments and pilots to leave that drunken L in the bulkhead and to fall spent on the floor beside me. The wonder of it is that nothing seemed to be damaged. Its companion shards had made a sieve of the bomb bay, but I did not know that then, so my memory is of that little hole.

The bombs were gone from the bomb bay when that flak burst came. Otherwise we would have been blown into oblivion by it. When the number four engine dropped off its mounts I opened the bomb bay and jettisoned the load. I wanted desperately to drop them through the doors and be done with it but I didn't dare. A trailing door would reduce our speed still further and make us more vulnerable, and we needed every bit of speed we could muster. With the bombs gone we took the flak burst without any vital damage. It came before the doors had completely closed, but it did not stop their closing.

I remember thinking sometime during those minutes of heaviest attack that, if we should all be killed, I would have to write letters of condolence to all those wives and mothers. The incongruity of such a thought escaped me at the moment. The possibility of my own death was considered only in the general "we" of the whole crew in which I could function as a part of the total organism while simultaneously maintaining my own existence as an individual. Thus, if we the crew should die it did not necessarily follow that I the individual would be free of the obligation to condolence. It scared me because I did not know how to comfort the bereft.

Somehow during the flight we found ourselves fighting for survival. There was no single occurrence that stood out as the turning point, no event which proclaimed "you have gone too far." There was only an osmosis of knowledge upward from the gut that time had run out. And with it came the steel set of mind that we would not go without leaving a good account of ourselves. I really believe that a well-trained crew has a being of its own, that it is an organism, and that the individual members respond to the needs of the whole without discernable communication. At least we seem to have reacted that way. We became an animal at bay, waiting with taut muscles for the last possible moment to strike, inflicting the maximum damage while conserving our own resources as much as we could.

But the time came inexorably. In a flying sieve with a gaping hole where an engine should be and another prop acting as a drag because it would not feather properly, with an upper turret warped off its track and the tail gunner unable to use his guns because they were trailing in mid-air, clinging to the rest of the ship by imagination and a wisp of metal -- in these conditions and with half the control cables shot away, it became obvious that we would have to abandon ship. We were alone now, the rest of the formation having long ago disappeared ahead of us, and even the enemy fighters had left us for more dangerous game.

Only the flak guns kept up their steady barrage.

When the order came to bail out I suppose that I reacted as quickly as anyone else, but my memory is of immense, deliberate concentration. I had been drilled so often in my responsibilities in case of emergency that my only thoughts were of the destruction of the bombsight and Mickey set. I felt the hard, sharp tug of the chute pack being snapped onto my harness but I did not see the navigator do it, for I was concentrating on the placement of the magnesium bombs and could not spare the time to adjust it. I took the consequences later in an uncontrolled parachute fall, but for the moment all of my concentration was centered on insuring that we would leave no secrets to be unearthed in triumph by the Germans. I was aware of the opening of the escape hatch, more a sensing of the changed atmosphere than a literal knowledge of the act, and I saw shadowy forms in the tunnel while I struggled to set the last of the magnesiums on the Mickey set, but the idea of using the escape hatch myself did not occur to me. I was an automaton going from task to task, making mental marks on an internal check-list.

When all my tasks were done and I could think of myself again, I realized that one parachute strap dangled unfastened and that the whole harness hung loosely on my frame. If I jumped in that condition I would slide through the harness and become a living bomb, arching through space on a trajectory that would bring me at terminal velocity to -- I sat in the tunnel and began pulling each strap into adjustment.

My progress was slowed by the erratic spinning and buffeting of the aircraft. I was slammed against the bulkhead by centrifugal force one moment and suspended in mid-air the next. I did not know that the wild gyrations were manifestations of a life-or-death battle between the pilot and an airplane hell-bent on self-destruction. I thought I was alone. So I struggled to get that harness adjusted before I gave it a final test.

It seemed to be half an hour later, but was no more than a minute at the most, that the plane leveled out and stopped its pitching and bucking. I marvelled to myself that it could have set itself so to rights, and wasted no time while trying to finish my harness adjusting. But I could not get that dangling leg strap fastened. As I fought it I felt a hand on my shoulder and knew that I was not alone. I went out the hatch into the blast of frigid air.

Always I had feared that escape hatch. It was so small that I found it necessary to turn my shoulders corner-to-corner in order to pull myself in through it. (It was the normal entry to the nose compartment.) And I always pushed my chute pack in first because I could not fit my frame in through the hole otherwise. I worried that, if I should have to use it in an emergency, I would not be able to get out through it with my chute on. But when the time came in earnest I went through that hatch with square yards to spare.

That a slice of time so small can contain so many currents of thought and sensations has always been a marvel to me. The elapsed time from my leaving the hatchway to being completely clear of the ship is infinitesimal, yet my mind was a drum-roll of do's and don'ts overlaid with worry that the belly guns might have been left down, and that in turn was overlaid by the thought that my chute might not open. And there was an accompaniment of mental checks of the other things I had done. All of this was going on simultaneously in my mind, each thought occurring at its own level without interfering with any other thought, and all progressing at their own speed.

I saw the bulk of the airplane pass over me and was dimly aware of another human form beneath it and knew that we were both safely out. Holding my left arm tightly across the chute pack on my chest I pulled hard on the ripcord with my right hand and felt the pressure of the drogue against my arm. Now my chute would open when I relaxed the pressure. If I should faint from lack of oxygen -- I had abandoned my mask when the order came to bail out -- at least I would not plummet into the earth without opening my chute. The flak guns might get me but I would have to run that risk. Before I could work up a good worry over that, I passed out.

Seconds later my mind cleared and my grip relaxed as my lungs screamed for air. As the drogue chute leaped out from the pack I turned to fall head down. I wanted to take the shock of the opening chute on my shoulders, thinking to avoid any possibility of slipping through the harness. I hadn't considered the whiplash effect this would have. When the canopy caught the air and snapped to its full-open spread I was instantly reversed and the force of the reversal cracked every joint in my body. Now, I know the persuasiveness of the medieval rack.

To be suspended in midair with only a silken canopy to support you is a sensation that defies description. You hang, not uncomfortably, with no sensation of movement or of wind. The sounds of the earth beneath you seem distant but have a clarity that is startling. The sound of guns is somehow intermingled with the trilling of a bird, the frightened squawk of a chicken with the sputter of a motorcycle. You are motionless, yet the earth beneath you moves gently to and fro.

The sound of guns -- suddenly I became aware that guns were still firing below me and that there were wicked black puffs above. I was in the line of fire, or maybe I was the target. I didn't know which and I didn't wait to find out. I grabbed the shroud lines with both hands and pulled hard. The forward edge of the chute collapsed and my harness went slack for a moment. Then the chute refilled. But in the process I had come noticeably nearer the ground.

It had worked so well that I did it again. There was the sudden sense of weightlessness as I fell free, and then the tightening of the harness as the chute again bit into the air. Feeling rather pleased with myself I looked up at the canopy, only to find that I was looking down instead!

Down! I was swinging through an arc that took me, at its peak, dangerously near to falling back into my own chute. One more tug on the shrouds and I would fall to earth in a flutter of silk. I tried to stop the wild gyrations but my efforts only served to add a spin to what was already a sickening oscillation. The unfastened leg strap made it impossible to control the chute, so I gave up and waited for my fate or for the motion to subside, whichever came first.

And I wasn't sure which I wanted to come first. The violent motion had made me sick; viscerally, desperately sick in a way that air sickness had never affected me. I wanted to vomit, to empty my stomach of everything in it, but nothing would come up. I hung limp in my chute and wished that I could die to be done with it, and I swung inexorably back and forth and around and around as I slowly dropped nearer the ground.

I was still swinging when I hit the ground. Those last few moments saw the sense of motion, which had seemed suspended when I first opened my chute, suddenly spring to life so that the earth rushed up at me like a train coming head-on. Everything was blurred by my motion and I could not see precisely where I would land. And I was aware that I was being carried along, too, by a spanking breeze that was going to make it hard to dump that chute.

Then I hit. Hard. It was new-plowed ground, bedded for the spring planting. Not only did I land cross-wind, but cross-furrow too. I took the shock of the landing on one leg and collapsed, trying to roll toward my chute. But the force of the landing took the breath out of me, and the plowed ground made it hard to spill the air. Gasping for breath, I was being dragged over the furrows like a cotton-picker's sack at day's end.

I had not seen her there although she must have been working in the field from the start. But suddenly she was there and her strong hands gathered in the silk as she strode over the furrows toward me. As she released the pressure on the shrouds I unsnapped my harness and shrugged it off, trying to stand up. My knees buckled and I was saved from falling by her quick grab of my arm. We stood there, my weight half supported by her sturdy grip, while a uniformed German rode his motorcycle over the bumps toward us.

"Brrr-umpphf! Brrr-Umpphf! Brrr-Umpphf!" The motorcycle alternately purred and grunted as he forced it diagonally across the furrows toward us. As he bumped to a stop in front of us she held out the bundle of silk and cord wordlessly. She had said nothing to me and she said nothing to him now. She just held out the parachute in a gesture that acknowledged his authority. He rapped out some guttural command to her that I did not understand and motioned for me to mount the motorcycle behind him. Whatever it was that he said stirred her to speech too, for she erupted into verbal fireworks. Then I understood her help to me. It was more than just compassion, for the stream of invective that she poured on his unmindful head was all in French! As we rode through the hedge and onto the road she was still clutching the parachute and shouting imprecations at my captor.

As the motorcycle puttered through the silence

of the countryside I took stock of my situation. I was deep inside Germany, not sure of my precise location and, judging from the pain beginning to make itself felt in my left leg, not in too good condition either. But I was alive, and my captor seemed to be trying to make it easy for me to stay that way. He was armed, but his pistol was holstered on his hip beneath my hand and the knife he carried could be slipped out of its sheath before he could act to stop me. At any secluded spot along the road he could be mine.

But he knew more than I gave him credit for. At no point in our ride were we ever out of sight of others. Always there was the crew of an anti-aircraft gun, or a detachment of Home Guards, or some other armed group within easy hailing distance.

At one point where the road cut through a small woods we were stopped by a troupe of *Hitler Jugend*. They were a strapping lot of teen-aged kids in *lederhosen*, showing their new-found masculinity in boisterous activity, cradling their rifles self-consciously. Their leader, a little older perhaps than their twelve and thirteen years, and certainly bigger than the others,bounded down the embankment to discuss the situation with my captor. His HJ shirt, with all its decorations and shoulder patches, was a bit too small for his shoulders and his *lederhosen*, obviously having served several older brothers before him, were ready to be passed on to the next. They were so tight in the crotch that he seemed to walk with a wince as if in a state of constant sexual excitement.

He and my captor exchanged a few comments, the one showing the bravado of youth and the other an amused tolerance. I didn't understand any of it, but I did not miss the hard cold hatred in the eyes of the blond youth when he looked at me. Nor did I fail to see, as we pulled away, the gesture as he spat contemptuously in our direction. I shuddered to think what my fate might have been had he and his crew of adolescent thugs got to me first.

As I said, we were never alone. For quite some

distance we puttered along with a small military convoy until it came to a stop near a gun emplacement. And other traffic came and went, never giving me that one chance I needed. If I had got it I don't know what I would have done. I had no real knowledge of my location except that I was somewhere west of Berlin and east of the Rhine. And my chances of making my way back out of an occupied Europe were just a dream.

I had not yet learned to recognize the different German uniforms, but I have been eternally grateful since that my captor represented the *Luftwaffe*. I was to find that there was a sort of chivalry which required that one airman treat another with respect even when they were on opposing sides. And that fact operated to my advantage when he deposited me at the city jail in Burg. I could not understand his conversation with the jailer, but he repeated "*Luftwaffe, erst Luftwaffe*" several times and I took it to mean that I was to be released only to the *Luftwaffe*. And, as it turned out, that was exactly the intention.

Much later I learned of men who fell into the hands of civil authorities and were held for months before they were permitted even to leave their cells. Others who were captured by less humane captors than mine were given over to the *Gestapo* for non-stop questioning for days on end. It was that point in the war when the German economy was being beaten to its knees and the natural reaction was for them to strike back at any symbol that came to hand -- at any symbol of the Allied air raids which were a constant reminder of their predicament.

He had been my captor, my escort, and, in a sense, my security on the long ride into the town. And I felt a sense of loss at seeing him go. I remembered the *Hitler Jugend* in the woods and wondered if I had got past one bad situation only to fall into another.

Burg

The jailer was an old man, wispy with age, bald except for a close-cropped fringe, and palsied. His hand shook so badly that he had trouble entering into his ledger the fact that he was accepting me from the *Luftwaffe*. Him I could overcome any morning before breakfast. He didn't even wear a gun on his belt and as far as I could see, there wasn't one within the tiny cubicle that was his office. But my captor stood in the doorway, blocking any exit. And he stood there until the old man had opened the iron door of a cell, motioned me in, and then closed and locked the door. Then he repeated his injunction of "*Luftwaffe, erst Luftwaffe*" and was gone. I heard his motorcycle sputter to life and purr away down the street in the direction from which we had come a few minutes before.

The old man tottered back to his cubicle and busied himself with rustling papers and closing desk drawers. I could not see him and had no idea what it was that he was looking for until the pungent odor of strong tobacco came drifting into my cell and the rattling of drawers stopped. He must have saved all the cigarette butts he could find and supplemented it with hay to get such a stench. But he settled down to enjoy his pipe and I, in my turn, settled down to inspect my new surroundings.

The jail was a primitive place with great thick masonry walls that could easily be relics of the Middle Ages. From the street we had come through a tiny entry hall into a bare room. It had no furniture at all, only a dim electric bulb dropping from the ceiling. Its one window was heavily barred and too dirty to admit much light. That was the only dirty window I remember seeing in that town, but it was dirty enough to make up for the rest. The jailer's cubicle was walled off near the front of this room, apparently having been enclosed as a relatively modern afterthought.

A door at the rear of the room gave onto a dim and narrow hall that, at first glance, seemed to be interminable, but it was only the dimness that made it seem so. As my eyes became adjusted to the light, or lack of it, I realized that the corridor gave access to four tiny cells. It seemed long because the end walls were plastered over with unpainted cement, a dull gray color that faded into the general gloom and seemed to disappear. The rest of the walls showed some sign of having once been painted but those two end walls were bare.

The cell itself was barely eight feet long and not more than four wide. Its only furnishing was a wooden platform swung on chains against one wall so that it could be let down to form a bed of sorts. The only light came from a tiny window set high in the rear wall and heavily barred. I don't know how high the ceiling was but when I stood on the bed platform and reached up to the window I could not see out. I grasped the bars and pulled myself up, hanging only on the strength of my own arms, but all that I could see was another stone wall a few inches away from my window.

I let myself down and tried pacing the floor, but a four by eight foot floor does not lend itself to pacing and my leg was getting more painful, too. I sat on the bed and tried to relax, but that didn't work either. I tried reading the graffiti scratched into the stone walls but it was all in German. I wondered idly what one did about the call of nature in such a place --there was no toilet facility in the cell and none was visible in that part of the building I had seen. Not that I needed one just then, but the thought did occur to me that it might prove difficult to explain to the old man.

My thoughts were interrupted by sounds from the front of the building -- sounds of someone coming into the entry. I heard the old man push his chair back and knock out his pipe against the tile floor, then there were voices going through the same general conversation that had been the changing of my keepers. I heard him rustling his papers again as he entered the new admission in his ledger and then the sound of footsteps as he steered the new prisoner into the hall.

There was a sharp catch in my breath as I realized that the new prisoner was Len. He had come out of the hatch behind me and I had seen his parachute open, but after that I had lost sight of him in the maelstrom of my own uncontrolled fall and had no idea how far apart we might have landed. My first impulse was to shout aloud, to tell the world that I was no longer alone. And I might have done it had I not caught one instant of command in the look he gave me. It was just a momentary meeting of eyes yet it reinstituted all the months of practice when he was the commander and I the subordinate. It was a look that at once commanded silence and at the same time pleaded for it, and it worked. The sound in my throat died and I was able to return the blank look of two total strangers.

The old man locked him into the cell next to me and shuffled away, swinging his great iron key idly. I stood a moment at the bars that formed the door to my cell, tempted to speak yet knowing that I would not. I could not see him -- our cells were parallel, separated by a thick wall of stone -- but I could hear him going through the same exploratory moves that I had made. I stood a moment until the pain in my leg wore into my consciousness again, and then I let down my wooden bunk and stretched out on it.

Perhaps a village jail is not the ideal place to take a nap but my nerves had been stretched to the limit so long that I was exhausted. In spite of the situation and the mounting pain in my leg I fell asleep on the hard boards of my prison bunk.

I don't think it was a sound that woke me, but a

sense of being stared at by someone. At least, I was not conscious of any sound. As I came awake I saw the window high above me and the vaulted, empty ceiling beyond that. My senses strained to identify whatever it was that had awakened me while my eyes searched for someone, something, whatever it was that made me feel I was being watched. I arched my back and neck, seeing the world upside down in consequence. There, wide-eyed in wonder, stood an old woman and a boy.

I must have lived up to their expectations of a demon, a *terrorflieger*, a *morderish Amerikanisher*, for they stared open-mouthed for an instant and then fled. Their precipitate flight apparently was triggered by my sudden, uncontrollable laughter, for I found the looks on their faces, their fear of the caged beast to be hilarious. My howl of laughter sent them flying down the short hall and out through the main room without a pause. I heard the outer door slam as the old man scraped back his chair and shuffled in to see what caused the commotion.

It was quite some time later that I heard voices again in the main room and the grating of the huge key on its ring as the old man took it out of its drawer. He came alone into the corridor, unlocked both our cells, and motioned us to follow him. The thought raced through my mind that now was the time to tackle him, but the stamping of jack-boots in the outer room effectively chilled my ardor.

We came into the main room to find a uniformed and rifle-equipped German standing ramrod straight in the center of the room. I recognized his uniform as being the same as that of my original captor and thought to myself, "*Luftwaffe, erst Luftwaffe.*" I didn't know what it meant but I knew that the uniform was right, at least.

"Your name, please." He spoke in English with only a slight accent to betray his German-ness. We gave our names, trying not to look at one another, keeping up our pretense of having never met before. He waited while the old man laboriously entered our names in his ledger.

"Your serial number, please." The old man entered these, and then our rank – rating, the Germans called it. And he translated each to the old man. "*Zero, seben, funf, seben, neun,*" and so on through our serial numbers and ranks, repeating when the old man faltered.

Finally it was all done and the old man retired to his pipe while the new guard explained to us that he would take us to the *Luftwaffe* station near Magdeburg. He might as well have said Hong Kong for all the information it conveyed to me for I had lost all track of my location. But he methodically explained that we would have to walk to the railway station and there would be some considerable changing of trains and streetcars along the route. I think his intention was to impress on us the point that he felt at a disadvantage and might, consequently, get trigger-happy if we pushed him.

But his message was not necessary, for I was rapidly coming to realize that I was in no condition to push my luck. My left leg was now swollen from knee to toe and pain knifed through me each time I put my weight on it. I had often twisted an ankle before, but never so painfully as this. I wondered how I could walk to the railway station and what the guard's reaction would be if I fell along the way.

I need not have worried, for he let me set the pace and, when I faltered, he let Len support me. We kept up our pretense of being strangers but I leaned more heavily on him as we approached the station.

That matter of pretending to be strangers was something we had discussed long before, not really believing that we would ever be called on to carry it through. The idea was to deny the Germans any scrap of information they might conceivably put to their advantage. That included acknowledging what organizations or crews might be involved in a raid. If we admitted to being from one crew then they would deduce that only one aircraft was down, whereas, if we pretended to be strangers, they might go on indefinitely searching for a non-existent crew and aircraft. Anything that denied them aid was justified and anything that tied up their manpower was to be attempted.

When, at last, we reached the station I was ready to concede it was no mere sprained ankle with which I had to deal. I am a person with an exceedingly high pain threshold and, consequently, sometimes don't recognize my own hurts. But that one was not to be ignored. My foot and leg were so swollen that I could no longer tolerate a shoe and the merest touch was enough to make me recoil in pain. Without Len's help I would never have been able to keep moving.

On a series of interurban trains we zigzagged south. Always our guard managed to find a seat where he could sit behind us with his rifle across his knees or, when the arrangement of the car permitted, he would sit facing us with his back to the door.

Somewhere in the sprawl that was wartime Magdeburg we found ourselves on a streetcar with a short bench running longitudinally from near the conductor's enclosure to the first regular seat. Our guard appropriated this space -- the bench and the first seat -- by moving the civilian occupants to other seats and directing us to sit facing forward while he occupied the bench at right angles to us. It was an ideal arrangement from his point of view because he could see everyone in the car at a glance and could also see anyone entering the car at the numerous stops. But he too must have had a long and wearing day for he soon began to nod.

I had catnapped now and then along the route but the pain in my leg now made that impossible. Each time the car swayed on the tracks in the way streetcars do I would cringe with the shifting forces exerted against my swollen foot. I stiffened my body against the roll but that only gave added impetus to the surge and made my heel fall against the battered floor, adding the shock of a new source to the pain which was already intense.

Across the aisle from us a woman fidgeted with a string bag, searching through an assortment of groceries and undistinguishable personal items. I watched idly, not really seeing but aware of her movements. Having found what she wanted she clutched it in her hand and pushed the bag back to the floor. The car swayed again on the tracks and I tried vainly to avoid banging that perverse leg into the floor. As the car righted itself, a tiny corner of my attention was caught by her action. Had she leaned just a bit farther in my direction than the motion of the car would demand? Was her spontaneous grasp at the edge of my seat really so spontaneous? Through half-closed eyes I studied her, trying to discern if she was holding something in her hand or if it was simply closed by chance.

But she sat rigidly, staring toward the front, giving no apparent indication that she was aware of my existence. Then the car swayed again and, as I was swung slightly toward her, she opened her hand the tiniest bit, holding it low so that the guard could not see. She was not looking at me -- she stared straight ahead -- but she obviously was showing me that she had a scrap of paper in her hand.

As we rattled down the tracks I waited breathlessly for the next warped rail that would send us lurching sideways, hoping against hope I would be able to contact her hand and transfer the bit of paper to mine without anyone else seeing it. What did it contain? An address, perhaps? I had heard of the underground activities in Europe and even knew some who had been spirited out after being shot down, but this was deep inside Germany. Surely it was too much to expect to find clandestine supporters of the Allied cause here in the very heartland of *Hitler's Reich*. Yet there she sat with her bit of paper, waiting for the next warped rail, too.

But we were doomed to failure, for the guard suddenly stood, indicating that ours was the next stop. When the car came to a halt I braced my hands against the seat and pushed myself erect, balancing on my one good leg. As I teetered there, trying to gain enough equilibrium to hobble out and down the step, her eyes met mine for just one flash and I knew that the underground was indeed at work even on Hitler's doorstep. Painfully I made it down the aisle and swung myself out to the cobblestones. The pain was only partly caused by the damage to my leg.

There may have been runways hidden somewhere among the buildings but, if there were, I didn't see them. There was only the gatehouse and, behind that, the austere stone buildings which unmistakably bore the imprint of governmental bureaucracy. There was no mistaking the fact that this was a military encampment. The things that come to my mind now are the ever-present signs that said "*nicht rauchen*" and "*kein eintritt*" but I was not really aware of their meanings yet. They may not really have been there at all -- perhaps I only associate them with the place because it was so overpoweringly military.

My non-functioning leg gained us some extra consideration which I am sure we would not have been entitled to otherwise. We were escorted into a large, almost empty room by our English-speaking guard, who then left us to the custody of two very young and pimply-faced goons. (Goon was a term I had not yet learned to apply to our keepers but, in time, it became so commonplace that I wrote it without thinking. It was only when I read the sentence again that I realized that I would not have called them goons at the time.) There were no chairs in the room, only a desk pushed against one wall as if waiting for removal. I sat on the edge of the desk to relieve my aching leg, but not for long.

"*Nicht sitzen*!" His voice was not yet firmly settled into its masculinity and tended to squeak on the sibilant sounds like a fingernail against a blackboard. I didn't fully understand his words but his meaning was unmistakable: I was not allowed to sit on the desk.

"*Nicht sitzen*," he repeated, unslinging his rifle as if to enforce his edict. I didn't wait for the third time. I stood with both feet on the floor no matter what the pain. I had not survived this day to die at the hands of some adolescent kid who was probably more scared than I was.

We stood, not talking to each other, not really looking at each other, for what seemed an eternity. By unspoken agreement we carried on the charade of being strangers, hoping to confuse the enemy at least to some small degree. I had almost reached the limits of my endurance and was seriously wondering what the reaction would be if I fainted when a sergeant came bustling into the room. I didn't know his rank except that stripes on the arm mean sergeant in everybody's army, and he had stripes on his arm. Lots of stripes. And he spoke English.

"It is broken, yes?" His face showed genuine concern as he motioned me back to the desk that I had been ordered off of. I hesitated to sit there again, not wanting to be threatened again by the kid with the gun. But the sergeant patted the desk top, motioning for me to put my leg up.

"Sit, please. It pains? It is broken?" I sat on the desk and gingerly brought my leg up to rest more comfortably along the edge.

"It is badly wrenched, but I don't think it is broken. I have been walking on it. No, it isn't broken." I could feel the panic mounting as I realized that this might be a cause for separating Len and me, and suddenly I didn't want that to happen.

"Just a few questions and then we have the doctor see, yes?" He made it a question, yet it was a simple declarative sentence. It did not invite a reply and I gave it none. His face was kind, but something in his voice told me that he could be otherwise when circumstances dictated.

The special consideration I spoke about was the fact that he came to us, rather than have me climb the stairs to his office for questioning. I learned this later, too late to be properly appreciative. Apparently his concern for my physical state was genuine and humane.

He had brought a clipboard and sheaf of papers

in with him and he now began to ask those "few questions" and to write the replies into the spaces of prepared forms. He asked for name, rank, and serial number, of course. But he also wanted to know what organization we came from, what our home station was called, who our commanding officer was, and dozens of other things to which we could not, in good faith, give him an answer.

And he wanted to know if we were from the same crew. There it was, that justification for our pretense. We looked at each other blankly, hoping that our eyes would not give us away, and did not answer. He repeated the question, looking from one to the other of us, seeming to measure our reaction. We returned his look with what we hoped was a noncommittal stare.

He shrugged his shoulders and rasped out an order to one of the adolescent guards who were standing stiffly near the door we had entered. The boy leaped into action as if from a catapult. He stalked across the room, the hobnails of his boots ringing sharply against the stone floor. With both hands he grasped the handles of a pair of double doors and flung them wide. His action had a quality of play-acting that would have looked overly theatrical even on a stage. But its result wiped the thought clear of my mind.

There they stood, staring open-mouthed at us -- the rest of our crew. There was that one moment of absolute silence, then the war whoop as Earl realized that we were indeed alive and there present in the flesh. The others joined in and surged into the room to talk to us. The German sergeant calmly filled the last blank space on his record.

It was the first time, but certainly not the last, that we were entrapped by the German passion for infinite detail. Their knowing that we formed a single crew served no useful purpose, yet they had gone to the trouble to assemble us in this way to prove what they must already have known beyond a reasonable doubt. And it very effectively blew our charade. Len and I could now recognize our mutual past and stop the pretense. We no longer needed to hide our thoughts behind poker faces, or try to.

They had thought we were dead. When they left the plane, eight men in rapid-fire succession, they had watched as they hung suspended in air, waiting for our chutes to show. They had witnessed the death throes of the craft and, at last, just before it disappeared entirely into the distance, had seen it nose over and dive into the ground. There had been no evidence of any more chutes and they grieved to know that we two were a part of that last violent explosion that ended the dive. They had watched the aircraft so intently that they never saw our chutes opening several thousand feet below it.

The sergeant's voice cut through the bubble and hum of the reassembled crew's conversation. It raised again that moment of panic at the thought of being separated from my one contact with the known.

"You must go now to hospital," he said to me in English before turning to the theatrical guard with a guttural stream of what was obviously very detailed instructions.

I don't recall how I got from the interrogation room to the hospital but I must have been helped at least in part by my guard for my leg would no longer tolerate a touch. I may have gone hopping on one leg or I may have been half carried by the kid; I really don't know. But somehow I crossed the open ground between the rows of buildings and entered another room devoid of furniture. But this time I was not made to stand and wait. We were met at the door by a strapping young lad who appeared to be a hospital orderly and I was unceremoniously lifted and carried into an examining room.

I lay for a long time on the examining table, trying to make my muscles relax, trying to avoid that feeling of panic, of being alone in a hostile world. My guard sat beside the door with his rifle across his knees, trying to look properly impassive and serious, but more often succeeding only in looking like a little boy playing at being a man.

Outside the windows the last shreds of daylight faded into that gloom that is night without real darkness, the murkiness that is a spring night in northern Europe. Somewhere someone flipped a switch and the bare light bulb above me glowed to life. I heard footsteps in the hallway now and then, but otherwise there was no one there but my guard and me. I felt a gnawing hunger and realized that I had gone without food since an early breakfast back in England. And so much had happened since.

At last a doctor came. I must assume that he was a doctor although I can't be certain, for he spoke no English and I was in no position to question him. But if he was not a qualified doctor he was, at very least, a most compassionate man. His examination was gentle, his touch delicate and apologetic for the hurt it caused. He felt for torn ligaments and moved my toes about in a test for something that I did not understand.

He brought a bit of gauze and a mask like a funnel from a side cupboard. From another he brought a bottle of clear liquid. Ether, I thought. He arranged them carefully on a little wheeled table that already contained several other medications and instruments. He opened the bottle and its smell permeated the room at once. It was not ether, but I could not identify the odor. Lowering the gauze-filled mask over my nose and mouth, he trickled a few drops of the liquid into the gauze.

"*Une, deux, trois,*" he said as he looked at me with questioning eyes. Then he moved his fingertips lightly across the soles of my feet. My toes curled at his touch and I winced from the pain, but I had no idea what he was saying to me.

"Oon, do, twa," my brain said, and it made no sense at all. It didn't have the harsh, guttural sound that I had come to associate with the German that I had heard all that day. But it made no more sense, either.

"*Une, deux, trois,*" he repeated, then his face brightened and he switched to another series of sounds.

"*Ein, swei, drei,*" they came harshly to the hearing by comparison to his previous crooning. But they were no more intelligible. His fingers again touched the soles of my feet and I was startled to find that I felt it, not in my feet where his fingers were, but somewhere up in my legs as if my feet did not exist any longer.

"*Une, deux, trois. Ein, swei, drei.*" His voice, his eyes, his whole being seemed to be pleading with me for something. His fingers moved restlessly across my soles as I tried to comprehend his meaning and the sensation of his touch moved ever higher. It was as if I were dissolving from the feet up. I could see his hands moving across my feet, I could see my bare feet there at the end of the examining table, yet the sensation of it was above my knees now.

"*Une, deux, trois. Comptez, s'il vous plaît. Comptez!*" The sensation was in the pit of my stomach now and my vision was becoming blurred. My eyes seemed not to be able to focus any longer, creating weird double images peopled with moving shapes without edges. And my thoughts were becoming jumbled. I seemed no longer in control of my own being.

In one last flash of clarity before the anesthetic took over completely the insistent "une, deux, trois" resolved itself in my mind. How simple! How could I have been so blind? He wanted me to count aloud so that he would know when I was asleep.

"One, two, three." I counted aloud. My voice was weak and quavering, but it was enough to let him know the state of my consciousness.

"Four, five, six." My throat felt as if it were closing and my tongue was thick, but I got the words out. His smile was beaming with each word.

"Seven, eight, nine." My voice faded until the last word was inaudible, but my lips still moved. He smiled encouragement and stroked my feet again. I felt nothing.

"Ten, eleven, twelve." No sound came, and

even the movement of my lips seemed to have ceased. My eyes focused on his face and wandered away without my being able to control them. One moment the world would be in sharp focus and the next I would be plunged into a visual void.

"Thirteen, fourteen, fifteen." I counted on, although all sign of consciousness must have left me. He waited at the foot of the examining table, just a shadow now in a world of shadows. When my count reached forty I sank into a restless but total sleep.

I swear that it was the snap of his fingers that woke me. Like a side-show hypnotist he snapped his fingers and I was instantly awake. I have related this to a few doctors since then and they invariably raise their eyebrows and tactfully avoid comment, not wishing to call me a liar. But I clearly heard the sound, and for hours afterward any sharp cracking sound would rouse me from sleep.

My leg was swaddled from toe to knee in a plaster cast. I could feel its weight and its rigidity, but I could not see it. My eyes seemed to be completely beyond my control. I could see clearly those things which should have been in my peripheral vision, but dead ahead was a void. I was frightened, not so much by the heavy cast as by the limiting of my vision.

Pushing myself upright on the examining table, I swung my legs over the side while I twisted and turned my head to get a look at what had been done. It was an awkward thing to tilt my head sideways and down in order to see what I should look at straight on. But there it was, a neat cast that rounded out just below the kneecap so that I would be able to flex my leg at least a little. And the pain that had grown steadily worse throughout the day had ebbed somewhat.

I saw the cast, but I also saw that the orderly was back — the one who had carried me into the examining room. His stocky form was visible by the door when I tilted my head and turned ninety degrees away from him. He stood where the guard had been earlier and, as best I could determine with my wild and blurred vision, he was the only company I had in the room. I wanted to ask him what was wrong with my eyes. I wanted to scream out to him to help me see, to give me back the sight I had always had. But something kept me from it. I sat tensely, waiting for the next move.

He seemed to be in no hurry, moving about the room now and then as he tidied up some of the mess left from whatever had been done to me. He picked up bits of gauze and plaster where they had fallen to the floor and polished a table top where some liquid seemed to have spilled. I followed his movements as best I could and was surprised to realize that half my sight really was hearing, that I heard the bits of plaster scrape against the floor as he picked them up and heard the slight swish-swish of his cloth on the table top. I saw the gross motions, but I heard the fine-tuning. It was something of a consolation to realize that blindness would not be a complete cutoff from the world. A very small consolation, but a consolation nevertheless.

A sound at the door caused me to look in that direction, forgetting for a moment that my eyes did not work that way. I stared into the blackness, then turned my head enough to see another man wrestling a stretcher into the room. He laid it on the floor and braced it open, chattering all the while to the first orderly in a language that eluded me. My ears were so tuned to hear German that I could not accept for the time the fact that this was something else. As it turned out they were speaking French, but I didn't realize it until much later.

They lifted me bodily and laid me on the stretcher, not unkindly but with a firmness of self-assurance. The big one looked at me and laughed to see my feet dangling a good twelve inches over the end of the canvas. He shifted me a bit to shorten the overhang and make it possible to lift the stretcher without bumping into my broken foot — by now I was willing to concede that it was indeed broken — and laughed again as he made some comment to his companion. It must have been funny for they both were still giggling as they hoisted me and carried me out into the corridor and started up the stairs.

"*Futbol*?" It was a question he directed at me and it was oddly accented, but it very definitely was intended to inquire if I were a football player. I thought at the time how odd it was that he, who looked like some college linebacker with his massive shoulders and bulging muscles, should think me a football player. The few pounds I had spread over my long frame would never pad me against the rough-and-tumble of the game.

I laughed and shook my head, trying at the same time to get into position to see his face. But, with my limited field of vision combined with the slant of the stretcher as they carried me up the stairs, it was impossible to see what his reaction was. I had to content myself with trying to grasp the tonal meaning of the stream of conversation between the two of them. Besides, I was getting very sleepy and my mind was beginning to wander off.

By the time they got me to a bed in the ward I must have been thoroughly unconscious again, for I don't remember even reaching the top of the stairs. But it was a drugged sort of sleep that was broken now and then by sounds -- any sudden sharp sound was enough to bring me awake, only to drift off again in a few minutes. Each time that I awoke the big orderly would hurry over to try again to engage me in conversation. Sometime during the night my brain cleared enough for me to realize that he was speaking French but I could not concentrate well enough to try to make sense of any of it.

When morning came I was ravenously hungry. Breakfast in England had been a very long time ago. Someone brought me a thin slice of black bread spread with a tasteless, oleaginous topping that I took to be some sort of jelly, and a tin cup of scalding hot coffee.

"*Ist ersatz*," someone said to me. I didn't know what the words meant and I could not see the speaker, but I took the food eagerly and began to eat it. The bread had a bitter tang to it and the coffee tasted like pure tannic acid, but it was food and I was badly in need of it.

As I ate I tried to listen to the sounds of the ward and see what I could of it in an effort to sort the whole thing out in my mind. It appeared to be a ward in the station hospital, for there were no guards that I could discern anywhere and the other patients seemed to be German. At least I thought that they spoke German. The orderlies alternated between French and German, but the patients spoke commandingly in German. So they had put me, unguarded, into their own hospital! Did they not realize that I could overpower other patients and kill them before they could get me? Didn't they know that I could -- but who was I trying to kid? What would I kill anyone with, my tin cup? Or my cast, perhaps? I finished my coffee and went back to sleep.

Sometime in midmorning the big orderly came back with a pair of crutches for me. He was followed by an armed guard who made it very clear that he expected me to use the crutches as soon as I got them adjusted to the proper height. So I was escorted downstairs and out into the open. Since I could not see very well it was slow going, but eventually we made it out past the guard shack to the trolley stop where the rest of the crew stood with a motley collection of other crews and guards. The move to the interrogation center had started.

Der Bahnhof

Dulag is a word not included in my German dictionary, but it is a very real German word. Perhaps it is a combination of some other word with "*lager*" just as *Oflag* is a combination of "*offizieren lager*." At any rate, *Dulag* was the name given to the interrogation center at Oberurzel near Frankfurt-am-Mainz. It was a collection center where all prisoners, that is, all American Air Corps prisoners, were gathered for brain-picking and brow-beating before being sent on to permanent camps.

We were on our way to *Dulag* and had just arrived in the station at Frankfurt when the air raid siren sounded. Mind you, this was no pleasure jaunt we were on; we were some fifty or sixty men who had been assembled in Magdeburg and had been brought this far with almost as many guards. They seemed to feel that we were likely to break out at any moment and go rampaging through their cities.

Our progress across Germany had been a cramped and uncomfortable sort of thing, crammed into the tiny compartments of a train with only just enough room to sit if everyone sat bolt upright. The guards stood in the corridor, one on either side of the compartment door. If anyone stirred inside, their gun muzzles jerked instantly to point at the offender and to demand absolute stillness.

Of the eight or ten people in one compartment two of us were wearing leg casts while a third was bandaged from the waist to the top of his head. Only his eyes showed through the layers of gauze and when he spoke the bandages slipped and wriggled so that he was constantly adjusting them to cover the burns on his face.

These physical restrictions -- the bandages and the casts -- made it difficult to maintain the sort of stillness that the guards seemed to demand; consequently, we were under almost constant threat from their rifles. And, after hours of menace without action, it became a hollow threat. We came eventually to ignore the pointed rifles and the guttural commands which we didn't understand.

The man with the bandaged face and chest would appear to be the most badly wounded of us all, but he seemed not to be in any pain at all. He carried on animated conversations, extending his efforts even to trying to talk to the guards. He was not successful as a rule, but he tried with each change of the guard.

The other man with the broken leg, on the other hand, appeared not to be in bad condition at all. Whereas I had boarded the train painfully and slowly, pulling myself up carefully on my crutches so that I would not lose my balance and fall, he had come bounding up the platform on his one good leg and a single makeshift crutch. And, in the first hours of the ride, he had seemed to be in exceptionally good spirits.

But, as the hours wore on and the tension of such close confinement grew, he became more and more subdued. He and I sat facing one another on the window side of the compartment. I suppose that arrangement was arrived at so that we would not have our casts bumped by the others as they shifted position. We sat with our legs and crutches interlaced in the narrow space between the seats and stared at nothingness, for the blind was closed tightly over the window and we were not permitted to open it for even a moment.

At first the change was visible only in that he talked less and the muscles of his face seemed to harden into a mask, as if he were straining against some internal pressure. Then his color began to take on the ashen look of pain and he shifted his leg frequently to ease the tension. And he began to tremble in little recurring spasms as if the most intense pain were ebbing and flowing in a tide. Then his eyes closed and his head fell forward, rolling with the motion of the train as if he were asleep.

I felt a sense of relief that he was able to sleep and wondered vaguely if someone shouldn't tip his head back so that he wouldn't bob and weave. My thought was cut short by the sudden gasp and rasping sound of his breathing that made itself heard above the clack-clack of the train. His body stiffened into rigidity, his back arched away from the seat and his legs probed far beneath the mass of other legs and crutches. I leaned across the intervening space and felt for his pulse.

It was wildly erratic, pounding at trip-hammer speed at one moment and dropping almost to nothing the next. Shock! I don't know how I knew it, but something told me that he was on the verge of shock. Probably some first-aid lecture of long ago had suddenly surfaced in my memory when I needed it most. Everyone moved off of the seat on that side of the compartment and sat on the floor so that we could get him into a prone position. They sat crowded against the knees of others and held him down when the worst pains would make him writhe and twist in agony.

The guards shouted and waved their rifles about but we ignored their threats, concentrating instead on trying to help the poor man through his crisis. We begged the guards for a doctor or a corpsman, for medical attention of any kind, but it did no good. When they would not respond to our pleading in English we tried using other languages, French in particular, but that only brought grunts and threatening gestures. None of us spoke German at the time, but we were certain that the word "doctor" was essentially the same in that language and that our guards could not fail to understand the need for one under the circumstances. But they chose not to understand. And the spasms came more frequently all the time.

Then his pulse stopped, his breathing ceased, and we held a corpse in our arms. He lay still at last, death having eased the pain that had made his features look hard and old, leaving him now no more than a boy defeated by forces beyond his understanding.

We continued to sit, too stunned to act even if action had been possible. And I think we may have wept a bit at the loss of one of us, although we were strangers before that day began.

But we did not reckon with the indomitable spirit of the man. Slowly, imperceptibly, the knowledge came that he was breathing again. At first I thought it was my mind playing tricks. The tiny lifting of his chest must be caused by the motion of the train. But, no, it came in a slow, steady rhythm that was not related to our surroundings. It was weak and hardly noticeable but it was there. I felt his pulse again, feeling that I was being a fool, for corpses do not have pulses. There too I found the weak but steady evidence of life.

We waited for the terrible spasms to return but the boy slept peacefully, his heart and his lungs gaining strength with the passing time. By the time the train reached Frankfurt he was able again to sit up and, when the air raid siren sent us underground, he was carried by two of his able-bodied companions in spite of his protests that he could make it on his own.

Underground meant the sub-basement of the main railway station in Frankfurt. We were hurriedly moved from the platform down a long flight of stairs, along echoing corridors and through empty storerooms, until we came to the last narrow stair that led to the very bottom level of the cavernous building. There we were held up a moment while someone searched the place to be sure there were no escape hatches, I suppose, and then we were moved single file down into the darkness of the cellar.

The air was damp and the stone floor cold, but an English-speaking guard made us sit, each man braced against the knees of the man behind him, arms overhead to protect against falling masonry. As much of the station as I had been able to see as we came across the platform and down through the building did not seem to have been damaged by the war, but it was obvious that the Germans feared that it would be the target this time.

And they were right. We could not hear the aircraft overhead but we could feel through the earth the vibrations set up by the firing of anti-aircraft guns. The single bare light bulb that dangled from the ceiling seemed to dance about on the end of its wire in response to the mad tempo of the guns.

The first bomb explosions came with the intensity of an earthquake. The walls trembled and plaster fell from the ceiling in a shower that pelted us like sharp-edged hail. The dim light wavered, flickered out, then came on again in a surge that gave a momentary brilliance to the dust-filled air. A few moments later it went out for good, leaving us in the clammy darkness amid the crash of more bombs above our heads.

What had started as identifiably separate explosions soon resolved itself into one continuous pounding against the ear-drums, the diaphragm, the sinuses. All the empty spaces, the sounding boards of the body, were subjected to intolerable and constant pressure. The masonry rained down in a torrent on our heads and the dust swirled in choking clouds.

I felt rather than heard the racking cough that seemed to surge back and forth over the fabric of bowed heads. As the dust thickened the coughing became more frequent, sending tremors along the lines of close-packed bodies, seeming to reverberate through the blackness of the chamber. And the pounding seemed now to be concentrated directly above our heads.

I don't know how long we were suspended in that hell of blackness, noise, and dust, but at last we became aware that the pounding had stopped. I don't think we heard it so much as felt it; our hearing was impaired to the point that we no longer heard anything. But we found that the earth no longer trembled and the plaster no longer fell about us. The dust continued to swirl through the air, leaving our lungs seared and gritty although, in the blackness, we could not see it.

People began to move out of their cramped positions, some standing and others just moving their limbs about to relieve the tension. In the total blackness these things were perceived but not seen, sensed through the momentary touch of a hand as someone stood or the brush of a leg as it was moved about. And sound returned, very slowly at first, with the half-heard barking of the coughs that built until I knew that I could talk and hear and be heard.

And still there was no glimmer of light and no evidence of our guards. They had been there when the light went out but, if they were still there, we could not hear them. People began to feel their way along the walls, hoping to find some means of escape back to the world of air and light and life. I thought of the tomb scene from 'Aida' and wondered if we were sealed into our own tomb. I thought of the strangely silent and missing guards and wondered how they had gotten out of the cellar, or if they were still there.

Someone realized that our guards might have been killed by falling debris and that some of our own men might have died also. So we felt our way around the cluttered area, feeling for yielding flesh in the sharp-edged masonry.

We were engaged in this task when a flashlight beam suddenly shattered the darkness above us. Its beam flicked quickly around the dust-filled room and them settled on what remained of the stairway. And the voice of our English-speaking guard from the trip down ordered us to come up in single file.

There was never any explanation of what had happened to the guards but they obviously had survived the attack, for they stood ranged along the pathway out of the cellar, and their grim faces told us not to try anything now. It was no time to tempt one's fate.

As we came up out of the dust-filled cellar the moon struck clear and bright on the scene of devastation around us. What had been a vast and busy railway station a few hours earlier lay now at our feet. We had gone down an endless flight of stairs, along an echoing corridor, down again, and then at last down the narrow steps into the cellar. We walked back up an endless pile of rubble. Of all the massive stonework that had made up the building only the ceiling directly over our heads had held intact. All else was in ruins.

In the half-light of morning we were marched out through the tangled rail yard to the open country where we again boarded a train for *Dulag*.

III

The Crew
And Other Personalities

We formed as a crew in Utah and traveled together to the plains of Texas to begin our training. That is, the bulk of the crew formed in Utah; we had no co-pilot nor navigator until our training was almost ended. But the pilot, the gunners, the engineer, and I trained together during those long winter nights and dust-filled spring days. We drilled each other in emergency procedures and practiced alternating positions until we each knew all the essential jobs of the crew. While we might not qualify as experts in everything, each man was capable of bringing the ship home if he had to do it under emergency conditions. We could all fly it at least passably, and we could all navigate at least enough to get us home. Every man knew how to arm the bombs and how to jettison them if need be. In short, we became an all-round qualified combat crew.

In the process we developed lasting friendships. Stewey, who often doubled as our co-pilot after serving in the same position for his own crew, was accepted as if he were assigned to us. Major Cool, our training group commander, became a sort of foster father figure. Because I attended so many of the navigators' briefings (in the absence of an assigned crew navigator) I was accepted among the navigators as one of them although my knowledge of their craft was rather skimpy.

Major Cool

His name was Kuhl. He pronounced it "Cool." And that is how we thought of him, as Major Cool. He was our group commander and a genuine hero from the early days of World War II. He had been one of the last to evacuate Clark Field before it fell to the Japanese.

We were young air crews in training. We had been assembled as crews in Salt Lake City and brought to this desolate strip of Texas panhandle to practice the flying, the bombing, the gunnery that would prepare us for actual combat. Two years of warfare had not brought the Japanese nor the Germans to their knees and our services were urgently needed overseas. So we dropped sand-filled bombs on target ranges. We flew long, boring navigational flights to sharpen our skills. We fired countless rounds of ammunition into sleeve targets, pretending they were attacking aircraft.

But there were also days when the weather would not permit flight training. Such days were rare, but they did occur. And when they did, Major Cool felt we should have something to occupy our minds and keep us out of trouble. The ground crews, of course, still had work to be done and were, therefore, not a problem. But our duties consisted of flight training and, when the weather would not permit flight, we were at loose ends.

His solution was to assemble the entire group in the briefing room for lectures from men who had experienced actual combat. He wanted us to understand that war was not a great adventure, but a bitter battle between men where no quarter was asked nor given. That was his intention.

The result was something else. Each lecture soon disintegrated into a story-telling session which had no relation to the original intention of training. Men who had seen combat tended to want to talk about the lighter moments of life in the war zone. They did not want to remember the bad times. And so the training lectures, good as the original intention was, became entertainment instead.

And Major Cool himself was the most entertaining of the lecturers. He had flown a B-17 out of Clark while the entire base was under attack by the Japanese. He took off for Australia without a full gas load, knowing that he probably would not make it to Darwin but hoping that he could set it down on a beach somewhere without too much damage. If he managed to nurse it all the way to Darwin another airplane was saved for the war effort. If he didn't, at least the Japanese had been denied another plane and crew.

But he really didn't talk much about the flight. It was the unintended consequences that he remembered and enjoyed recounting. His gas tanks ran dry somewhere over the eastern Timor Sea and he had to ditch the plane near a small island. He hoped for friendly natives but could not be sure the Japanese had not got there first. And in the ditching, he and several others were wounded slightly. His navigator, however, broke a leg, a serious wound which might hamper any attempt to make it to land. There were sharks around.

The natives were friendly. They swarmed out in their outriggers to ferry the crew to land. A "coast watcher" radioed their location to the authorities in Darwin and they settled down to wait for rescue.

And when it came, it came in the form of a submarine. Airmen and submarines are not a good mix. Men who have never felt even a twinge of airsickness tend to become seasick easily. Major Cool's navigator was a classic example. From the moment the sub submerged until it surfaced again outside Darwin harbor he was seasick - violently and exhaustingly seasick. In addition, he had picked up a bug from the native food on the island

and it gave him a severe case of diarrhea.

With a broken leg, diarrhea, and seasickness, he found it impossible to go to the bathroom alone. Someone had to help him down the companionway, open hatches for him and, finally, flush the toilet for him. Toilets in submarines have a unique problem: the pressure outside is greater than the pressure inside. If you do not pressurize the contents of the toilet first, the whole procedure works in reverse: the sea flushes in instead of the toilet flushing out. Pressurizing the toilet involves the simultaneous turning of several valves while pressing levers with the feet.

As an aircraft commander without an aircraft Major Cool felt a particular responsibility for his men. He assigned himself as helper to the navigator. He was certain he could manage.

They had been at sea for less than an hour when Joe had to go to the head. That's bathroom in navy talk. Major Cool helped him down the companionway, through the hatches, and into the head. There was not room for the two of them to be in the head at the same time, so the major waited outside the hatch. When Joe was ready for the toilet to be flushed he rapped on the bulkhead and they traded places - Joe outside the hatch and the major in the head.

Major Cool had read the instructions very carefully. He knew exactly which valve to turn in what sequence. He was sure of it. He closed the toilet lid and pressed his foot on the left lever. He turned the upper valve to the right while turning the lower to the left, just the way the instructions said. And then he put his foot on the right lever.

Whoosh! The lid flew up and the contents sprayed across his uniform, fouling both him and the entire head.

Only after he had got himself and the head cleaned up did he see the fine print: "Caution: release left lever before depressing right."

Tommy

Tommy was a tall kid. About six feet. Broad shouldered. Good looking. He had a mop of black curley hair that defied the regulation GI buzz cut. If he had not been in uniform you would have thought he was someone's fourteen year old kid brother. He had the face of a choir boy. He hated it. Little old ladies thought he was cute and wanted to mother him. He wanted to be accepted as the nineteen year old man that he was.

Tommy and I were roommates when we were cadets. Everything was done alphabetically. "Shallich" followed "Rogers" on the roster, so we shared more than just our room. We sat next to one another in classes. We marched next to one another in formations. If he carried the guidon at the Saturday parade, I was right guide. If I carried the guidon, he was right guide.

And we were partners in flight training as well. We were assigned as students to a specific instructor, but he was over-worked and couldn't possibly make all the flights with all the students assigned to him. Consequently, we sometimes flew our training missions without an instructor. Just the two of us with a pilot and a bomb bay full of practice bombs. One of us would drop half the bombs while the other filmed the results. Then we would switch places and repeat the process.

We had a good working relationship. But we were not very proficient at bombing. Often, after one of those flights without an instructor, we would find that our scores were terrible. We knew they were terrible. We had seen the bombs landing hundreds of feet outside the center of the target. And we had the film to prove our incompetence.

We didn't do much better when we had our instructor along. He would try to show us what we were doing wrong, but it just didn't get through to us. We were both lousy bombardiers and well on our way to being eliminated from the program. "Washing out," it was called. There didn't seem to be anything we could do to prevent it.

Periodically one of us would be called up for a "check ride." That was a practice mission flown with a special instructor whose purpose was to evaluate your capabilities and decide whether you could stay in the program or would be eliminated. Each time we would manage to squeak by with the minimum rating. Our self-confidence was being slowly whittled away. Our youthful enthusiasm turned to pessimism. We conceded to one another in private that we were just not going to make it. The only good part of it was that, when the elimination came, we would be given the rank of staff sergeant. At least we would not have to start at the very bottom.

Our "week end" was Thursday and Friday. There was a war on and everything was being juggled to fit a training schedule designed to provide the maximum number of combat-ready men in the shortest possible time. One week end, when our morale was at absolute zero, Tommy and I went into town. We had nothing on our minds except that we wanted to get away from the base, away from everything having anything to do with training. We rode the bus into town and then walked aimlessly from one store to the next, looking at merchandise we had no use for, pricing items we knew we couldn't afford. But it was something to occupy our time and to take our minds off the inevitable - the absolute certainty that we were going to be eliminated from the cadet program.

In a jewelry store we looked at watches. Neither of us needed a new watch. The army had issued us perfectly good watches as part of our necessary equipment. And we couldn't afford any of the ones we looked at. But it was a boost to the ego to be treated as if we could. I'm sure the sales lady knew we were not going to buy, but she treated us as if we were very important customers.

Lying in the display case among the watches was a selection of brooches and pins. One of them caught my eye. It was a replica of a bombardier's wings, complete with the miniture bomb on the circular shield designating "observer." But the wings were studded with small, clear stones. I assumed they were rhinestones. I asked to see the pin.

Tommy was immediately caught by the piece. He asked what the stones were, thinking they might be small diamonds.

"Oh, they are only rhinestones," the salesgirl said. "But arent't they pretty?"

"Very nice. But how much does it cost?" Tommy was getting far too involved in this. Neither of us could afford to spend money on something which would probably have no relevance in a few days.

"It's thirty five dollars." The girl laid the pin gently on the glass top of the display case, seeming to carress it as she did. Then she picked it up again to gently polish the stones with her finger tip.

Thirty five dollars. That was half a month's pay. And for something we didn't need? I made excuses and hurried Tommy out of the store.

Out on the street Tommy gave me an accusative look. "You didn't have to push me out the door. I wasn't going to buy it. I just thought your mother might like it if we make it to graduation."

Later, as we wandered through the aisles of a five-and-dime store, I overheard two elderly ladies as they discussed someone else. Then I realized it was Tommy they were talking about.

"I do think a uniform looks good. The boys all look so smart in them," one old lady commented, under her breath.

"Yes. They do," the second one whispered. "But that one is just a baby."

Just a baby! I almost laughed aloud at the thought. It was hilarious that they would think him just a baby. I couldn't wait to tell Tommy what they said.

But Tommy was not amused. He was furious. He wanted to go back to find the two women and tell them that he was not a baby, that he was a man doing a man's job and doing it well. Only the fact that he was probably going to be washed out the next day kept him from following through.

It was a trivial incident and should have been forgotten. But it was a breakthrough of sorts in our gloomy thoughts about our future. Tommy seemed to feel a new need to prove himself, to show the world that he was indeed a man and capable of doing anything another man could do. His bombing score improved measurably. It was as if he willed the bombs to fall on target. The danger of elimination receded steadily.

I admired his determination but I could not match his performance. I still continued to hover on the border of disaster. It seemed that, every time I was scheduled to fly, it was for another check ride. Somebody seemed to want me to fail. Yet each time I managed to just get by. It was wearing my nerves to shreds. I didn't sleep well. I began to find my mind wandering in ground school classes.

When I finally accepted the fact that I was a failure, that I was going to be eliminated from the class, I reached a decision. If I had to go I would do it in grand style On my next flight I would drop bombs wherever they wanted to go. I didn't care if they landed in New Mexico or Texas. It made no difference to me where they landed. If I was going to be washed out anyway, I would give the authorities good reason for doing it.

In that state of mind I made my next flight. Once again it was a check ride. The instructor was not one I was familiar with. But that made no difference to me. I wanted to drop those ten bombs and be done with the whole thing. On the first pass over the target I set the course, checked the drift through the bombsight, cranked in a little bit of a correction, and sat back to see what happened.

The bomb dropped cleanly to the center of the target. I couldn't believe it. On the intercom Tommy yelled, "You hit the shack!" He was so surprised he wasted several feet of film because he forgot to stop the camera.

That first one had to be a fluke. On the second run I took a little more care but still made very few adjustments. Again the bomb went dead center on the target. I was in shock.

Time after time my bombs went into or very near the center of the target. When the tenth bomb left the aircraft I had become a bombardier. I was no longer just a kid trying too hard to master a complicated instrument - I was an accomplished technician.

On the week end before we graduated Tommy and I were again in town with nothing in particular to do. We would become second lieutenants on Sunday afternoon. In the meantime we had a lot of free time. We wandered again into the jewelry store. The rhinestone pin was still there, conspicuously displayed in the center of the case of watches. Tommy looked at it a long time. "I think you ought to buy it for your mother," he said. "She would like it."

I bought it. And when my mother died at ninety seven, it was still one of her special possessions.

Tommy died over the Ruhr Valley in 1944. He had no children. But, if he had had a daughter, I would insist on giving the pin to her. It really was Tommy's all along.

Len

Len was older than the rest of us, and more settled in his ways; more mature, as befitted his position of aircraft commander and pilot. At twenty-eight he was beginning to lose his hair and the corners of his eyes were beginning to show the permanent crinkle of maturity. Oh, he was as ready as the rest for a party or a joke, but he seemed to weigh the consequences a bit more carefully and often reined in our high spirits in time to save us from our own folly.

He was a methodical man. He was obsessed with the idea that we must be interchangeable as crew members, and he labored away day after day in the effort to mold us into that image. I seemed particularly inept at handling the aircraft controls, but he patiently went through the procedure time after time, trying to give me the feeling of the sweep and grace of a Fortress in flight. I was more attuned to the delicate adjustments of a bombsight, where just the pressure of a fingertip was enough to alter the apparent motion, and I found the comparatively gross movements of the control column and pedals threw me into a state of constant overcontrol. He would watch with narrowed eyes as I wrestled the great, flapping bird over half of Texas, then, with the patience of the truly dedicated, he would take the controls to show me how it should be done. He never criticized -- he explained.

There was that night when we had been out for an unusually long training mission and the whole crew was dog-tired, looking forward to home base and rest.

We had picked up a spare co-pilot who needed some flying time, but the navigation had been left up to me. Not that it bothered me to be called on to do the navigation -- I had used the mission to give the radio operator some training in dead reckoning. It was part of our policy of every man being interchangeable. But it left me drained of energy, having spent most of the time with my oxygen mask dangling while I shouted instructions into his ear. I was ready for some ground time.

As we came in toward the base I collected my maps and charts and headed through the tunnel to the radio room. It was not advisable to be in the nose compartment during landing -- in fact, it was strictly against regulations. As I came up to the flight deck I saw that the co-pilot was not in his seat and I popped my head in for a moment to see what was going on. As I did so, Len motioned for me to take the vacant seat and wiggled the controls in an invitation for me to take over. As I settled into the seat and fastened my seat-belt he leaned across the console and shouted into
my ear:

"How about making the landing tonight?"

It was not an unusual request, and I thought that perhaps it would be a good thing to get the feel of the thing at night like that. I had never landed a B-17 at night, but I was certain that it could not be very much different from daytime. And I had made many night landings in the smaller T-11. I flipped him a thumbs-up sign and took the controls.

Over the long weeks of practice my original wobbly control had settled into a sort of compromise with the airplane -- I still tended to over-react, but at least I did it more confidently now. So I brought the ship through the pattern, losing altitude in the prescribed way and controlling my airspeed so that I would be able to hit the ground just at stalling speed or a bit above it. I thought from his reaction that Len was very well pleased with my performance.

I cut back the throttles a bit more as I angled in toward the runway, getting myself braced to flare it out just at the proper moment and bring it down. Already I could feel the satisfaction of the perfect landing that this was going to be.

Then he did it. He slapped his hand across the console and cut all the power to the engines. I was still in the air with no power and no time to do anything but bring it in dead-stick. Instinctively I tipped the nose back down from the flare that I had just begun, letting it fly itself to the ground. I knew it was going to be one whale of a bounce now but it was too late for worries. I gripped the control column and hoped that the second landing would not do us in.

I could have saved myself the worry for Len was following my every move. He sat with his hands on the control column and his feet on the rudders, feeling each movement and ready to over-ride or remedy any error. As we touched down and then bounded into the air again he let out a whoop that was pure exultation.

The second touch-down was beautiful. The gear kissed the tarmac and clung. Slowly the tail settled until the tail-wheel touched too and the whole craft seemed to nestle onto the runway like a great swan. Len revved the engines and we taxied in.

My novitiate was over. As Len put it over a late supper, anybody who could dead-stick a B-17 onto the ground with only one bounce could do anything he wanted with it. After that my over-control never bothered me.

Len had a tendency to worry about things -- like the fact that we did not get a navigator assigned until we had almost completed our crew training. He felt the responsibility of his position as a crew commander and expected me to share in it to the extent of giving the navigator a check ride after he was assigned. Mind you, I was not rated as a navigator and had not had very much training at all in the use of the sextant, but I had been a part of the crew from the beginning so, to Len's eyes, I was qualified to observe and report. Sometimes I wondered what would happen to the poor guy if I said he was no good.

For a number of reasons that check ride never seemed to satisfy Len. Each time that I would report to him that the guy had handled a certain situation extremely well, Len would find something else that needed to be checked before we started overseas. And the upshot of it all was that I was still checking and Livy was still proving himself on the flight across the Atlantic. I think that Len finally accepted him when we hit the coast of Iceland dead-on in spite of the wildly incorrect weather report we had been given.

Earl

Earl was a mountain man, tall and rangy, with a slow smile that turned up the corners of his mouth and made the light in his eyes dance. He loved machinery of any kind and airplanes headed his list. He didn't love a plane the way a pilot does, for the things he can make it do; he loved it for the things he could do for it. Although we had no regular plane assigned to us during our training, he spent hours on end replacing safety wire, tweaking up the tuning of this or that, or just checking control cables and surfaces. He regularly inspected the bomb racks before each mission, even though I had already done it myself.

Like Len, he had a streak of worry in his makeup. As crew chief and upper turret gunner he was the ranking enlisted man on the crew, and he wanted to be included in anything that affected the other sergeants. Not the goodies -- he felt a genuine responsibility for the well-being of the others and went out of his way to try to help in situations that were really personnel matters.

Bit by bit I came to know him during the months we spent in training, but he was constantly bringing to light new facets of his character that I had never seen before; like the night on the train when we were headed north to pick up our gleaming new B-17 to fly it to Europe. We were not ordinarily a hard drinking crew -- that is, we drank, but not as a matter of course. Special occasions called for a drink but just run of the mill drinking was not usually our way. This must have been a special occasion because someone had brought a bottle aboard the train and we had sat sipping it from paper cups as the train clacked and clattered across Oklahoma.

It had been a long day and, one by one, the men turned in until, at last, only Earl and I were left with the bottle and the tail-end of a conversation that someone else had started. And that soon died for neither of us was really interested in it. I was feeling a little lonely and frightened at the thought of going into combat, and I suppose that he was too. We sat, staring unseeingly out of the window as the black night rushed past, sipping the raw tasting liquor and trying hard to like it.

"Hell, I'll never see them chickens!" He said explosively, with the accent on "see". I must have looked startled by his outburst, as indeed I was, for he chuckled and looked away, half hoping that I wouldn't ask what chickens.

"What chickens?" I couldn't resist so incongruous an opener. I had to know what he meant.

"Them chickens I bought last week," he said. "Had a hundred of 'em mailed home to Mama. Won't do no good, though, 'cause I won't get home in time to see 'em fryin'." I had never known that he kept up his interest in farm activity. Of course he was a farm boy, as most of us were. But we didn't send baby chicks home to be raised. This was a new facet to me.

And it lead to many more. As the train rattled and creaked through the night he talked, hesitantly at first but more volubly as the night and the liquor wore on. He told me his plans for the future, of the house he would build on his own mountain top, of the livestock he wanted to raise, and of the girl he wanted to marry. This last came as a revelation for he had never hinted to anyone that he might be considering marriage. In fact, we didn't even know that he had a steady girlfriend. Most men carry a picture of the girl, show it around at the least provocation, but it was only after a lot of talk and some persuading that I got him to dig out the picture from his wallet to let me see it. She looked a lovely girl and I have never understood why he was so reluctant to let the picture be seen. But that was Earl's way.

Earl's way could also be profane. On that last mission when we were fighting for our lives he took a twenty millimeter burst in the base of his upper turret, a burst that warped the lower plate so that he very nearly couldn't use it at all. The shock of it threw him out of the turret and sent him sprawling onto the flight deck. He picked himself up, climbed back into position, and banged away at anything that came within range of his crippled guns. He must have got his foot on the mike switch accidentally, because his swearing and pleading came through loud and clear on the interphone. He alternated between swearing at the fighters for not coming within his range and pleading with them to get a bit closer so he would have a better shot at them.

And he could be stubborn. When we were interrogated at *Dulag Luft* he refused to give even his name. We were bound by the rules of the Geneva Convention to give name, rank, and serial number, but that meant nothing to him. He stubbornly and against all advice continued to hold out long after the German interrogators had determined what they wanted to know. For hours on end the conversations would go like this:

Interrogator: "Goot morgen, sergeant. Vee vant some information from you for der records. Vhat is your name, please?"

Earl: "Screw you. I ain't tellin' you nothing'!"

Interrogator: "But, sergeant, vee only vant vhat is required. Vee do not try to trick you. You must give your name."

Earl: "Go to hell!"

Interrogator: "Vell, vhat is der noomer, der serial noomer?"

Earl: "Damned if I'll tell you."

After a while the interrogator would seem to lose his patience, shaking his fist in Earl's face, shouting at him while he stamped menacingly round and round him. His voice would rise to a crescendo as he threatened:

"You know what vee do to peoples vhat don't cooperate? Vee shoot dem. Vee don't know your name, vee don't know you are American. Maybe you are German saboteur? *Ja*, maybe you are German and vee haf to shoot you."

Earl was silent.

Then there would be another tack, a pleading for cooperation in the interest of the other prisoners, or a recital of reams of unimportant facts from Earl's past. This last was intended to impress the prisoner with the point that they knew all there was to know anyway, so he might as well answer their questions.

It was wasted effort. Earl continued to hold out even when the officers and men were separated and sent to different camps. As far as I know, the German *Luftwaffe* was never successful in getting him to admit to his own identity. He may be the only living Unknown Soldier.

Jersey

Jersey was a strapping lad, open-faced and eager to please; like a big, blond puppy, really. We thought of him as the baby of the crew because he was younger than anyone else, but that didn't really mean much; we were all under twenty-one except for Len. He was still a little bit uncoordinated and inclined to be all feet and elbows, but he was eager to learn and to do a good job of it.

His crew position was waist gunner. He had no other duties. While Earl doubled as engineer and gunner, and Oral as radio operator and gunner, Tom as armorer and gunner, Jersey had no second job. He was a gunner. But he aspired to be so many other things that it was sometimes difficult to keep up with his latest whim.

When his turn came to learn the essentials of the cockpit he spent hours going over all the various instruments, asking what they were used for and how they worked. And he dreamed of flying the plane, not just as a novice learning emergency procedures, but of flying it himself as a fully qualified pilot. It was only daydreaming, but he wondered aloud about his chances of going to pilot training. It did no good to remind him that there was a war on and we were slated to soon see action in it; he continued to live out his daydreams.

When I took him into the nose compartment to teach him the vital essentials of bombs, sights, and chin turrets, he fell in love all over again with the glamour of secret instruments and high explosives. The bombsight was still classified as a top secret device in those days and I think he saw himself defending its secrets from the whole of the Axis Powers. I had intended only to give him the essential information on how to get rid of a load of bombs in an emergency and how to destroy the instruments if that became necessary, but I found myself going into details of bomb trajectory, composition of explosives, fuse timings, and a thousand other things. Not that this was secret information; certainly it was not. But they were things that interested him and his interest was infectious. It would have been unkind to give him less information.

His curiosity ran the gamut from airplanes to curly hair. One weekend he joined me for a short visit to my sister in the oil fields of West Texas. It was a long trip by bus and we just had time to catch our breath before we had to start back to the base, but Jersey learned about curly hair.

Or rather Jersey learned how straight hair gets made curly. The females of his family had always had their hair done at a beauty shop and I don't suppose it had ever occurred to him to wonder just what the process consisted of, nor what it looked like in the curling. On the other hand, I had grown up in a family of girls who were their own beauticians and thought nothing of it.

So Estelle met us at the bus station with her hair in curlers with a turban covering it. Curlers then were not the bright colored plastic things that they are now; they were wire spring coils covered with a sort of mesh. The hair was wound around the coil and secured with a bobby pin or two. So they were not terribly obvious when covered with a kerchief or scarf. But they must have been uncomfortable to the wearer.

She lived "on the lease", as they say in the oil fields, which is another way of saying that she lived in a company house in a company development miles from anywhere at the end of a gravel road. As she drove expertly around the wandering cattle on that road I noticed that Jersey kept glancing at her hair, or at what he could see under the babushka. But she and I had a thousand things to talk about and I didn't really give him a second thought.

Later in the afternoon, after Estelle had disappeared into the bathroom and had come out again with her hair uncovered and all properly curled and combed, Jersey could contain his curiosity no longer. He had to know how the metamorphosis had been made, and so he asked. Ordinarily such a question would have been considered rude or, coming from a man as it did, at least most peculiar. But his open fascination kept it in perspective. And she gave it the attention it deserved. She laughed, of course, and she teased him a bit about not knowing how women were camouflaged, but she answered his questions.

She did better than that, really; she gave him a demonstration. While he watched in obvious fascination she put her daughter's hair in curlers and, after we had eaten and the proper interval of time had elapsed, she took the curlers out and showed him how limp blond strands had been turned into springy curls.

He was incredulous. As she combed out the curls to give them the proper "bouncy" look he would gently pull one out to its full length and watch it spring back into shape. And he shook his head and muttered over and over:

"I never knew that was how they did it!"

And that is how Jersey learned about curls.

Stewey

Stewey was not a member of our crew, and yet he was. That is, he was assigned as co-pilot for another crew, but he had flown with us so much in training that we felt he somehow belonged to us. In the days and months when we were training without our own co-pilot he often did double duty, flying with his own crew and then again with us in the same day. He was one of those men who simply can't get enough time in the air to please them.

He and I had found a mutual interest early, an interest that developed into a genuine and easy-going friendship. We enjoyed walking. Back in the States we often spent part of our weekend just walking through the town, looking at the houses and the people who lived in them. And when we landed in Ireland on our way to England we spent an entire day walking through the countryside with no destination in mind, just walking.

We were comfortable companions. Often we would go for a mile or more without a word passing between us. We had no need to talk just to make conversation; indeed, we were more often silent than not.

Our first real chance to see any of England came at Stone in Staffordshire. We were herded like so many cattle from Ireland to Liverpool and onto the train to Stone. Nowhere were we given the time nor, for that matter, the daylight to see any of the country we were passing through. But there was a war on, as we were constantly reminded, and we must hurry up and wait.

And that is precisely what we did. We rushed through the night to Stone so that we could wait for a week while the clerks and insurance sellers dawdled and piddled about the business of deciding where we were to be assigned. There must have been dozens of units in Britain at the time who needed replacement crews, but the paperwork had to be done properly before anybody could be assigned to any unit.

Stewey and I took advantage of the lull to see some of the countryside. At first we walked, just taking any country lane and following it to its end, or strolling through the villages that surrounded the base, having tea in a country inn, watching the people as they went about their business.

Then we discovered bicycles. The Special Services Section at the base had bicycles that could be checked out for the day if you got there early enough. You had to hurry to get one because there were always more customers than bicycles. But we were both early risers anyway, so we got there before the office was opened.

On our last free day we decided to go into Stone. Up to that time we had been wandering around mostly in the country and now we felt that we really should see the town before we were shipped out. So we mounted our bikes and pedalled away into town.

We rode for a while, moving methodically back and forth across the town, getting the layout of it and deciding what we wanted to spend more time seeing. There was the river with its arched stone bridges, and the street that seemed to be made up entirely of pastry shops. And there were dozens of shops selling strange merchandise. At least it was strange to a couple of naive American kids.

We left our bikes locked to a rack and strolled down toward the river. There seemed to be a great many people coming and going in the narrow street; so many that pedestrian traffic spilled off the narrow walks and into the street itself. There it mingled with the lorries and bicycles in a moving snarl. That was why we left the bicycles, really. We were afraid to ride them in that traffic. We tried to stay close to the shops, keeping on the walkway as much as possible.

"Psst!"

The sound could have come from any one of a dozen people in the vicinity. There was the old man who had just stepped into the street to give us right-of-way, but he seemed to be intent on his own thoughts. There were some boys who were heading home from school but they were oblivious of our existence, engrossed in their argument over who had won the soccer match. The woman pushing the baby carriage certainly would not have made such a sound, and I doubted that the two girls would have. I convinced myself that it was just a freak circumstance and turned my mind to other things.

We strolled on toward the river, trying to get a good view of the old stone span that arched above it. The press of humanity ebbed and flowed around us, sometimes forcing us to take to the street, sometimes leaving us almost alone on the walk.

"Psst!"

There it was again! And those same two girls passed us. They were walking briskly, swiveling their hips a bit more than the walking required, and trailing a strong scent of cheap perfume. I took a better look this time because it was so obvious that they were trying to attract our attention.

I would judge them to have been fourteen at the most. They had not yet learned how to apply their make-up smoothly. It lay in thick patches on cheek and lip, oily and livid; and their style of dress was somewhere between childhood and womanhood; the shoes were meant for adults, the dresses for girls. Their hair was piled high and held with cheap clasps. All in all, they gave the impression of two little girls who were playing at being grown-ups. We stood still and watched as they wiggled their way down the street toward the river. Then we laughed and took up our stroll again.

I saw them a few minutes later, heading purposely toward us, and I thought that Stewey saw them too. But perhaps he didn't, for he was deep into the logic of using keystone arches in building bridges. As they came nearer I saw that they were maneuvering so that they would pass between us and the shop windows. I had no idea then, and I still don't know, why the positioning was important to them but it obviously was, for they were bobbing and weaving in order to achieve it in spite of the crowds.

As they drew even with us I was watching intently to see what was going to happen, for Stewey stood with his hands thrust deep into his uniform pockets, facing the street, musing about the architecture of bridges. The girls brushed between him and the shop window, touching him slightly as they passed. As he leaned forward the nearer of the two leaned with him and suddenly spoke into the back of his blouse.

"Want to shack up?"

It was something less than a hiss but shrill and sibilant, as if braces on her teeth got in the way of her speech.

Stewey's face was a complete blank for a fraction of a second before he suddenly doubled over with laughter. And Stewey's laugh could be heard above the sound of the engines when we were in flight.

"What the devil is the matter with you?" I asked it even though I had heard the girl too, for they had slowed their pace abruptly, obviously waiting for an answer. His raucous laughter seemed to confuse them. It made it impossible for him to control the level of his answer and when it came it was a shout.

"Those kids want a shack date!"

Now it was their turn to look blank for a moment. They stood rooted to the spot a few feet past us as if this shouting to the world the fact of their proposal had left them powerless to move. Then they turned tail and ran, wobbling and bobbing in their unaccustomed high heels.

And everyone along the street joined in Stewey's laughter. A few of them even insisted on buying us a beer because we "taught the little blighters a thing or two."

Johnny

Johnny was darkly handsome, with the smoldering eyes, the broad shoulders, and the dark curly hair of the best of the Greeks. It was not his fault that women found him attractive. And his attractiveness was enhanced when he chose the company of Tom the Womanizer for most of his social outings. Together they made the rounds of the bars and dance halls of the local town, always with an entourage of adoring, or at least fawning, females most of whom were of somewhat dubious reputation.

Although they were not either one old enough to buy a drink legally, they never seemed to have any trouble getting liquor enough to bring them reeling back to the base at the last possible moment before curfew, usually accompanied to the gate by some of their most recent companions. Disentangling themselves there from the clinging arms and cloying kisses, they would make their unsteady way back to the barracks where they would regale the other gunners with fanciful versions of how they had spent the evening. It was always an entertaining story and no one really believed the whole of it.

But it never interfered with their duty. Next morning they would wake bright-eyed and eager, as if they had been waiting all night in anticipation of this day. And, in a sense, they were, for they were a happy pair who lived each moment to its limit and managed to spread some of their sense of joy among the rest of us.

Although we ragged him endlessly about leading Johnny astray, Tom's part in all this was essentially honest and innocent. It was simply that he preferred the company of what he referred to as "wild women" and both he and they knew exactly where they stood in their relations. There was never any doubt that Tom was the master of the situation at all times. Entangling alliances, to use the diplomatic phrase, simply were not permitted. When the evening was over it was over, and there could never be any looking back.

Not so with Johnny. Perhaps it was that he was less experienced or just more naive. Whatever the reason, he gradually came to be seeing the same girls weekend after weekend and his references to them began to be guarded and noncommittal. Privately he admitted to becoming more involved with one than he really wanted to. Oh, not that he had done anything irreversible; but he had let himself get maneuvered into talk of marriage.

That presented a serious problem to him. He had no desire to marry the girl. In fact, he had every intention of marrying his hometown girl when the war was over or when his tour overseas was finished. He brought his problem to me and I counseled honesty. Tell her the truth and then don't see her any more, I said, and that would be the end of it.

When the next weekend was over and we had assembled as a crew on the ramp waiting for the last servicing of the plane before a practice mission the gunners were kidding one another as usual about the conquests of the weekend. Someone asked Jersey if it was his mother he was dancing with last night and someone else told Earl that his girlfriend was nice, all three hundred pounds of her. And so it went, back and forth like that. But Johnny stayed out of the general banter and tried to avoid being idle.

"Boy, ol' Bess was after you last night! What have you got that the rest of us ain't?" Tom was trying to bring Johnny out of his moodiness by including him in the general teasing. But it only sent him scampering into the tail of the plane to check his guns one more time.

"Ol' Bess would leave you limp as a rag if you would just give her a chance. She's after your body, boy." Tom was still trying to snap him out of it as we hoisted ourselves into the plane and prepared for take-off.

That night in the crew mess, amidst all the chatter of tired gunners and the rattle of silverware on metal trays, Johnny self-consciously sidled over to me as I sat talking to Len. I had been expecting him to want to talk to me but I had not anticipated his obvious embarrassment about it.

"Sir, could I talk to you?" he said, mumbling a little so as not to be heard at the next table.

"Well, yeah," I said. "Sure. Sit down and start talking." I never liked to put these things off. If a member of the crew had problems I wanted to get them out in the open where we could do something with them. And I wanted Len to know about them. He was the crew commander and he should know about our troubles.

"It's sorta private. Could I come to the BOQ?" His tone of voice said clearly that he didn't want to discuss his private life where anyone else could overhear. And I even wondered if he meant to exclude Len.

"Sure," I said. "Come on down to the room when you are ready. I'll be there all night." I wanted to say "and so will Len" but I didn't. Something told me not to rush the situation, to let it happen as it would.

Len and I shared a four-man apartment in the BOQ. The two extra beds were waiting for the yet to be assigned co-pilot and navigator. In the meantime we had it all to ourselves. Two bedrooms and a sitting room, if you could call them rooms. They were really just cubicles partitioned to eye level in a rickety tar-paper shack. But it was home for the moment and it was not uncomfortable for the time and the conditions.

I was listening to records when his knock came. Ravel's 'Bolero' was just beginning its sensual, throbbing beat and I hated to turn it off so I turned the volume down and opened the door. As I did so Len stood up, stretched himself lazily, and complained about the music through a yawn.

"Can't stand any more of that music. Think I'll go down to the club for a drink." He picked up his hat and sauntered out the door as Johnny sat down nervously on the edge of a chair. Len's complaint was a bare-faced lie, for he had just commented a few minutes before that 'Bolero' was his favorite of all of the records in our joint collection. But he carried it off very well and Johnny looked relieved not to have to confide his secrets to anyone else.

The door closed behind him and Johnny sat silently thinking his own thoughts and listening to the music. It was building now towards that first climax, the drum insistently probing while the trumpets swirled ever higher in their pursuit of ecstasy. I waited, not wanting to hurry him into whatever it was that he wanted to say.

The music reached its crescendo. It shuddered and gasped and then began again the slow, insistent, building tempo that is at once so sexually explicit yet symbolically pure. He sat perfectly still, his muscles tensed as if ready to flee at the slightest movement. Only his eyes moved as the fires deep inside them showed the turmoil of his mind.

The music hit its peak, that great shuddering, discordant blast that is both gasp and sigh, and settled into exhausted panting. His eyes were tortured now and I'm not sure he was hearing the music at all. Not, at least, in the sense of really listening to it. He seemed to be absorbed into it while living again something from the past that hurt.

"Would you turn it off, please?" he asked in a voice that seemed to come from somewhere outside of him. And having started to speak he could not stop. As I reached for the controls to shut the record player off he plunged into the story that had him so upset. And on and on he talked, forgetting at times that I was there, trying to explain to himself how he had gotten into this mess, and trying to find his way out.

Boiled down to its essentials the story was this: "Ol' Bess" was after more than just his body. She wanted all of him. She was a woman approaching thirty with two disastrous marriages behind her and she seemed intent on a third. They had seen one another sporadically at first, drinking and dancing together whenever they happened to meet. Then, somehow, she had arranged to monopolize his time so that he was seeing only her while Tom played the field of all the rest.

He had taken my advice and had told her the truth, had told her about the girl back home and their plans to marry. He had even thrown in the information that they were both putting money into a joint savings account so that they would have something to start married life with. And he had thought that his efforts were paying off, for she soon stopped protesting her love and need for him.

She let him talk until he convinced himself that he had won. Then she played her trump card. In strident tones, searing hot with the passion of a woman betrayed, she denounced him as a man unfit to be the father of the child she carried, a child she swore was his though he declared it could not be. She raged and cried. She threatened and begged. She pulled out all the stops in what must have been a masterful performance. And in the end she won. He had come home almost convinced that he had indeed fathered the child. Just where and when he was not sure, and in the clear light of the morning it had come to him that it really didn't matter. No matter how much he protested his innocence, men everywhere would believe her when she said he was the father. He was trapped and now he knew it.

Having told the story, he sat in dumb misery, staring at the floor. The corner of his mouth twitched convulsively as if he might burst into tears at any moment, but he maintained a stoic control. I tried to console him. I told him I would do all in my power to help him, and I sent him back to his barracks relieved at least to have confided in someone.

As soon as he was gone I grabbed my hat and literally ran to the club to find Len. This was something that he had to know about, had to help me with. It was something that I could not handle alone. Should we start by telling the chaplain or the legal officer? Or maybe we should go to the commander first. Len would know what to do and I had to find him and get his help.

I found him quietly sipping a drink while he played out a hand of poker. He glanced up and smiled as I came in, then went back to his cards. When the hand was played out he scooped up his little pile of coins and nodded toward the lounge. Without a word I followed him and sat on the hard leather sofa ready to pour out my troubles and confusion to him. He smiled again, that reassuring father-figure smile, and opened the conversation with a question:

"What is it this time? Do we marry him off or not?"

He obviously knew more of the private lives of our crew than I had given him credit for, and his getting to the point so quickly took me somewhat aback. I stuttered and stammered in getting the tale out but, willy-nilly, I got it told. And I kept repeating my conviction that he was being taken for a sucker. When I had finished the story and my own pent-up emotion had spent itself, Len stood up and reached for his hat.

"Don't worry about it," he said. "She's working an insurance scheme. She thinks he won't come back, thinks he will never know that she's not really pregnant. And she'll get all his insurance. I'll take care of it. And he did. Next day he took Tom along with him to identify her for him, and he went into town. Tom said he had to wait on the sidewalk outside the cafe while Len went in to talk to her. He was gone a long time and when he came out again he didn't discuss what was said.

But ol' Bess found another job and left town soon after that.

IV

Kriegsgefangenen

The personalities of the prison camps were not the personalities of the crew. The co-pilot and navigator were virtual strangers to us and soon formed their own attachments. Len and I remained close, although we were not in the same combine and were sometimes separated in the press of moving from one camp to the other.

The enlisted men were sent to another camp entirely. After the initial interrogation at *Dulag Luft*, we did not see them until we were liberated and had returned to Camp Lucky Strike in France. (Can one actually return to a place he has never seen before? Yet it felt like a return. We had come back to American control.)

Because the Germans issued food stuffs in bulk - a pitcher of soup for six men, a loaf of bread for four, and so on - we formed "combines," groups of men who lived together, ate together, shared their lives and their labors. We parcelled out the chores of housekeeping and maintenance among ourselves. We cooperated in digging stumps from the compound so we would have fuel. We took turns at salvaging tin cans to make new cooking pots.

And, when it came to pulling the wool over the Germans' eyes, we became consummate actors, accomplished thieves, hucksters of the first water.

Oscar

Oscar was Jewish in a time when it was dangerous to be Jewish. Hitler's fanatical hatred of the Jews made it necessary to conceal one's beliefs lest they bring down the wrath of the German state on the head of the believer. And to openly practice one's religion was out of the question.

But he had been brought up a devout, if not Orthodox, Jew and he found it hard to forego the form and liturgy of his faith. He always remembered the holy days although he could not do anything to celebrate them. During the High Holy Days of Yom Kippur and Rosh Hashannah he was withdrawn and introspective, but he did not give in to his sadness completely; he continued to do his share of the cleaning and cooking and seemed to try to put on a happy look when he knew that anyone was observing him. But it was obvious that his heart was in the temple even while his actions denied it.

He was our cook for most of the time in Sagan. We had started out with the idea that we would rotate the duties, including cooking, so that everyone did his fair share of the work, but we soon found out that we were much better fed when Oscar did the cooking and managed the kitchen. He had grown up in a family of haberdashers and had started working in the store when still very young, so his skill was as much a surprise to him as to anyone. But he enjoyed it and the rest of us agreed to take on all the other tasks if he would just cook for us.

To appreciate the difficulty of his task requires some understanding of the conditions under which we lived. We were twelve men quartered in a single room just four meters by five meters. Our food consisted of the standard Red Cross food parcel items plus a very meager supply of staples from the German *Luftwaffe*. Our cooking had to be done on the top of a tiny tin stove intended originally for heating purposes. Our fuel, as often as not, was pine stumps grubbed laboriously from the compound. Sometimes we had a bit of coal, sometimes we didn't.

Oscar's genius came out in making bland or downright unpalatable things into something exciting, or at least into something that everyone would eat and enjoy. Once we were issued dry millet in a surprisingly generous ration and Oscar turned it into breakfast cereal in short order. Millet is a grain not generally used by Americans as food and its issue precipitated a flurry of talk around the compound about how best to use it. We all knew that the sour black bread the Germans produced both for us and for their own troops was made from millet flour and most of us could not conceive of any way to use the grain while avoiding that sour taste. But Oscar kept his own council and put the grain into a pot to soak overnight. Next morning we were served a breakfast of hot cereal with cream and sugar, a cereal that would stand the competition of most any of the popular commercial brands.

But sometimes his efforts failed in quantity if not quality. It was some time after the triumph of the millet that the Germans issued us dry barley. Oscar soaked it overnight and was preparing to cook it the same way when someone noticed that the top of the pot was pushed askew. We were hurrying out to *appell* when the discovery was made so Oscar dipped out the excess into another pot, added water, and pushed the remainder to a warm spot on the stove so that it would begin to cook while we were gone.

Appell that morning took no longer than usual and certainly we did not loiter in coming back to the room, for our breakfast should be just ready and waiting for us. What we found was our breakfast overflowing onto the stove and down onto the floor. Oscar had judged the amount of grain to use based on the amount of millet that he had found to be just right. But barley is not millet. Under the influence of the water and heat it had doubled and doubled again in size until each grain popped open in the effort to absorb more.

We mourned the loss of the food that spilled onto the floor, but we ate our fill that morning.

One of Oscar's triumphs was toast, but it required the help of an assistant to make it without burning either the fingers or the toast. He had discovered that the sour German bread could be made almost palatable when it was sliced paper-thin and then toasted. But toasting was a major problem. If it were done on top of the stove all other cooking had to halt while the bread was laid out in rows and flipped like hotcakes. So he devised a way of toasting it against the side of the little tin stove. We took turns being his assistant, holding the thin slices against the hot metal with a fork and racking up the completed ones along the back edge of the stove-top so that they would stay warm. It was hot and tedious work but no one complained, for the alternative was to eat the sour bread as it came from the cookhouse. And it gave Oscar time to devote his full attention to the rest of the meal.

There were two things Oscar gave up on; green death and blood sausage. Green death was the popular name for something that the Germans called *Kohlsuppe*, cabbage soup. It was a mixture of dehydrated vegetables and water with sometimes a little bit of meat in evidence, but never very much. It looked inedible and tasted even worse. It was part of the German-supplied rations and was issued in big metal pitchers that were scalding hot when they came out of the cookhouse, but always managed to cool down to tepid before we could get them back to our room.

Oscar tried everything to improve that vile looking brew. On one occasion he even sacrificed half a can of corned beef in an effort to make it palatable, but it was a useless effort. Most of us would have gone hungry rather than eat more than a few bites of it, and some simply could not keep it down when they ate it. Why the Germans continued to supply it was a mystery, for most of it was wasted. I always suspected that, during the dehydration process, some of the cabbage was being allowed to ferment before it was completely dry, accounting for the foul taste and gastric rejection rate.

And blood sausage, too, was high on everyone's list of least favorite foods. As prepared for use by the German army it was exactly what the name implies: congealed blood with just enough fat in it to bind it together. No seasoning of any kind was detectable in it, not even salt. Oscar first tried frying it but that wouldn't work for it simply turned to liquid. Then he tried mixing it with various things: oatmeal, bread crumbs, anything that might mask its real identity but still give us the food value that it undeniably contained. But everything turned out to taste like blood sausage in spite of all his efforts. The final solution of the problem was that those who could, ate it as it came from the cookhouse; those who couldn't, didn't. I was one of the didn'ts.

But I must give blood sausage its just due. During the evacuation of Sagan little Fritz, the guard, apparently survived on blood sausage and black bread. He carried a large stock of each in his knapsack and gnawed away at them at every rest stop. The only obvious result was to greatly increase what was evidently a natural tendency to flatulence. If the name of "the little fart" had been bestowed in jest in Sagan, it was earned in earnest on the cold march.

But that gets ahead of my story. Oscar's efforts to make life more bearable extended to the concoction of cakes and pies. We had no flour but he dried the coarse ends of bread loaves and ground them into a flour of sorts. When thoroughly dried and slightly parched it lost its sour taste and could be used in a variety of ways. Probably our favorite, or at least most frequent, dessert was a sort of cake compounded of dark flour, prunes, dried milk, margarine, and whatever struck Oscar's fancy at the moment, including *Doktor Freyling Zahnpulver*.

That last sounds like anything but a foodstuff,

and it was. It was a commercial tooth powder sold in Germany at the time and on rare occasions was issued to the prisoners. Rare occasions, like a visit by the International Red Cross representative. But it was almost pure baking soda so it was a much-prized and carefully hoarded item. Oscar used it to get some degree of lightness into his baking, and we brushed our teeth with water.

Another of his creations which always brought on a wave of homesickness was a chocolate pie. And this one, on the rare occasions when he could assemble the ingredients, really was very much like the real thing. He used the grated flour from English biscuits to make a crust much like an ordinary pie crust. Then he filled it with a mix of D-bar chocolate, sugar, powdered eggs and margarine. And he topped it all off with a whipped cream made laboriously from powdered milk. Probably I have left out some of the things that he put in, but you will just have to take my word for it that it was delicious and that it is not just in retrospect that it seems so. It really was.

Supplying Oscar with cooking utensils was a full-time job. The Germans supplied each man with a bowl, a spoon, a fork, a knife, and not much else. There were a few pots held in common by all the men in the barracks, but most of our cooking was done in containers of our own devising. Tin cans, carefully split open and smoothed out, served as the raw material for building pots, pans, ovens, and even entire stoves. One of the regular details on which every man served his time was splitting and folding tin cans. They were carefully saved against the day when one of Oscar's pots would get a hole in it and have to be replaced.

The splitting was done with the table knives supplied by the Germans, and this led to a constant battle of wits with the goons and ferrets who prowled the compound. Using a knife for such purposes was strictly prohibited so we went to great lengths to appear to be doing something else while really splitting tin cans.

Oscar could not bear to see anyone go hungry. There was a time when I got a bad intestinal upset that Doc thought might be my appendix, or it might be food poisoning. He didn't know. Certainly it was not from anything Oscar prepared, for no one else got sick. At any rate, I quite literally lay in a coma for hours after I had vomited up everything loose inside me. And when I finally came round I could not keep anything down, not even water, for three days. I was becoming seriously dehydrated before I finally began to keep a little water down.

And Oscar fretted and worried. At first he tried to tempt me by offering to make special dishes for me, but he soon realized that it would be a waste; I would only throw it up too. Then he began saving my part of the daily ration so that I could have a big feast as soon as the nausea left me. I kept reminding him that I was going to be in no condition to stuff myself but it made no difference; he went right on planning what he would fix for me when I got up again.

It was five days before I even felt an interest in food and a full seven before I got much of it to stay in my stomach. And then it was mostly a few bites of dry toast. But eventually I did come round to the point of feeling that I could eat normal food in
normal quantities. That was when Oscar brought out all of the hoarded food that he insisted was mine, all of the food that I would have eaten if I had been able. There were two cans of pâté and one of corned beef, cocoa, jam, all of the things that I would have been entitled to from the Red Cross food parcels as well as several potatoes from the German rations. I am not sure what he expected me to do with it, but he seemed genuinely disappointed when I insisted that the rest of the men should

Doc

Doc was not a doctor. He was a fighter pilot who had some pre-medical training. He left college when the war started and became a pilot. He was shot down over Belgium soon after.

Because we had no medical personnel available - the Germans didn't feel we were important enough to warrant assigning their doctors to prison duty - we relied on Doc's meager knowledge to carry us through any illnesses we might incur. And he did the best he could under the circumstances.

He was allowed conference privileges with *Luftwaffe* doctors in truly urgent cases, but he was on his own most of the time. He was given space in a *vorlager* building where he kept simple medical supplies, mostly supplied by the International Red Cross. But he had access to them only if a guard was present.

He could make house calls on sick prisoners but he could not bring his medications with him. If you had to take something periodically, you had to go to the dispensary in the *vorlager* to get it. And you had to go under guard. Consequently, most of our ills went untreated, even though Doc did his best.

Bob

I was closer to Bob, I suppose, than to anyone else in the combine; closer than to anyone else at all except for Len. When I first saw him I was certain that he was the man with the bandages on the train to *Dulag*. His face and arms were livid with the scars left by burns, scars that I was sure would be with him always. His hair was just coming back in patches.

But he was not the man from the train. It was over a period of many weeks and many conversations that I gradually got the story of how he came to be so hideously disfigured. And while I was learning it the disfigurement was fading. Not just in my eyes. It was quite simply fading. Very slowly over a period of months the livid scars faded until they were not noticeable at all except for one bright red patch above his Adam's apple.

His plane had been shot down over France and he had bailed out at such a low altitude that he did not have time nor space to maneuver his chute. The canopy had popped open one moment and he had hit the high tension electric line in the next moment. It had all happened so fast that he had not even seen the wire. He had felt the searing burn as he slid past it, but he had not seen it. The shock of it had caused him to lose consciousness.

When he woke he was looking up into the rafters of what seemed to be a barn. And to his surprise he found himself to be completely naked, the clothing having been ripped from his body in shreds. It lay in a heap at his feet and he himself lay on what appeared to be some sort of work table.

As he tried to take all of this in he was suddenly touched with cold as someone began to plaster his wounds with some kind of unguent. He recoiled from the touch but was gently brought back by a firm hand. Then the cold, oily paste again. He twisted about until he could see his tormentor -- or was it benefactor?

She was a powerfully built farm woman who was obviously at home in her own dairy barn. She stood solidly at the end of the table with a bowl of fresh, sweet butter in the crook of one arm. And even as he twisted about to see her, she continued to oil his wounds with the butter while she crooned softly to him in French.

As he reconstructed it later, she must have picked him up from where he fell and carried him into the barn. That would have been no small task for he was a gangling six footer. And she had cut his clothing from his body, leaving it in shreds and strings on the table and on the floor beside her. Then she had begun to apply the only burn remedy available to her: butter.

When the Germans came to take him away -- they had seen the plane go down and the chute that came out of it, so it was not a case of having to hunt for him — when they came to take him away she had almost completed her task of covering all the raw burns with butter. She screamed at them and made fluttering motions with her hands that clearly said: "Go away! I am not finished with this job yet." But they would not go away. She continued dabbing the butter here and there even as the Germans prodded him to his feet, and she stopped only when they covered his nakedness with towels commandeered from her milk kitchen.

The only burn that she did not cover was that one little patch above his Adam's apple.

As I said, we came to be very close to each other, close in the way that brothers are close. We argued bitterly with one another at times, but we always stood united when the argument was with others.

And we spent long hours plotting the archaeological dig we would make when the war was over. Somewhere we had read about the Enchanted Mesa in New Mexico, its isolated ruins on top and its lightning-struck path that no longer reached the rim. We were intrigued by the mystery of it, a mystery that was enhanced by the one indistinct photo we were able to find in the meager library.

We were not deterred by lack of information, however. We simply estimated the distances involved, the space available on top of the mesa. Our plot involved attempting to land a small plane on the mesa, using it like a glider and hoping that we could bring it to a controlled crash before it went over the edge. This would be the vehicle to get us and the essential tools for a dig onto the plateau. The other, less essential things could be hauled up from the desert below by rope as they were needed.

Why we didn't consider using parachutes I don't quite know. Perhaps our recent experience with that form of transportation tended to discourage it. But we spent hours determining what the wind conditions would have to be for us to land the minimum load, and how we would disassemble the plane and lower it to the desert on a cable sling. We even drew up a list of what equipment we would need and estimated what its cost would be.

What we overlooked was the fact that one determined man with a parachute and a mountaineer's rope could get there and back at far less expense and danger to himself. We were willing but not wise.

Over the long months while we plotted archaeological digs and improbable escape attempts our friendship grew stronger until we had reached that point where communication became almost non-verbal. It was that rare thing of two men who seemed to know intuitively what each was thinking, even when no words were exchanged. We were not always together; in fact, we each had a circle of friends separate and apart from the other. But we did spend a great deal of our waking hours together.

And later, when we began the long shuffling from camp to camp we spent more than just our waking hours together. In Nuremburg and on the road to Moosburg we shared our blankets at night in order to keep warm. We learned to fold them just so with the edge of one tucked under the edge of the other so that they formed a sort of sleeping bag. But it would only work when we pooled our resources -- one man's two blankets would not hold together to keep out the cold. So each night we put together our makeshift sleeping bag and both crawled in, to lie almost motionless through the night for fear we would disarrange the blankets and let the cold air in.

Long afterward, when the war was over and I had returned to the University, I went with my family one Sunday afternoon for a swim at Barton Springs. I had consciously tried to put all thoughts of my prison experience and associates out of my mind so that I could concentrate on my studies. I had not thought of Bob in weeks but, suddenly, there he was, standing in shallow water across the pool from me. He had his back turned to me but I had no doubt about his identity.

I called my wife's attention to him and told her it was Bob.

"It can't be," she said. "They are still in Maine."

"But it is." And I dived into the pool, surfacing a few feet short of where he stood. As I shook the water from my face and hair he turned to me as if he had known all along that I would be there.

And he swore that he had known it

Bud

Bud was our block chief. That is to say, he was the highest-ranking man resident in our building at Sagan. He was responsible to the German authorities for our activities and presence at *appell*, the twice-daily headcount. He was also responsible to the Senior Allied Officer for equitable distribution of food, for the health and general well-being of the men in his building, and for relaying any escape plans to the camp's Escape Committee before they were attempted. But escape plans are only incidental to the story of Bud.

He went down in France on the day that he was to have been married. Everything was ready, his leave was signed to be effective the following day, the bans had been published and the hall hired. He had just to fly that one milk run to France and then all would be finished and he could get married and go on leave.

All would be finished. That was true in a way that he had not anticipated. The combination of his own low altitude and a German's lucky shot combined to end his mission before he got to the target.

He didn't talk much about it during the months that we were in Sagan, at least not to me, but it was obvious that, to him, thoughts of going home meant back to England and his still waiting bride-to-be. Back to

America could come later. He dutifully relayed all of the escape plans laid before him, both those that had a fair chance of success and those that didn't, giving his opinion of each as he laid it out. Never once did he try to get permission to use a good plan for his own escape. But the thought was inevitable that he would like to.

I have no idea how many plans he devised for himself. Certainly he must have worked on several and on more than one occasion must have presented them to the Escape Committee, but no one ever accused him of having pirated their plan. And he never got permission to try one of his own.

His chance finally came as we were being moved en masse down through the open country from Nuremburg toward Munich with Patton's army pressing hard on our heels. We were quartered in barns at night, sleeping in the hay where there was hay and on bare boards where there was not.

In a particular barn, separated somewhat from the other buildings of the cluster of farm houses and barns that formed the village, Bud made the decision that his time had come to escape. The noise of Patton's tanks could be heard distinctly at night and he was sure that it would only be a day or two before the front lines would move past him, if he could just stay hidden. He must have discussed his plan in some detail with George, but the rest of us were, for the most part, left ignorant of it. We could not be accused of participating in something if we didn't know it was happening.

As for me, I knew only that he had made the decision. As I bent over our fire that morning, checking water for coffee, George walked past.

"Bud's staying," he said softly as he passed. It was a statement meant to do more than convey a simple bit of information. It was intended, and I understood it, as an order to put into effect our standard goon-fooling technique at *appell* that morning. I looked at Bob and he at me, but we didn't say anything. We knew what we had to do.

When *appell* was called we lined up as usual,

with a great deal of shifting and moving about. George took his place in front of the group as if it were normal. No one mentioned the fact Bud would normally be out there instead. Bob maneuvered himself into the front rank and I stood behind him, making certain that there was a wide space between me and the man on each side of me. It was not necessary to tell them that I wanted space for the fast shifting of bodies as the count was in progress; everyone understood instinctively what we were doing.

As the *feldwebel* came down the line, counting us off aloud, I stood behind Bob so that I would be counted in that row. Just as the *feldwebel's* eyes moved toward the next row, Bob sneezed violently, spraying the *feldwebel* and all adjacent space with his suddenly expelled breath. In the split second that his attention was distracted I moved to the left slightly and was counted again. And Bud had gained at least twelve hours time in which to find his hiding place.

He found it, but his time-table was off. He had anticipated that he would have to hide for two days, three at the most, and so had taken very little food with him when he hid under the deep hay of the barn. And he ate sparingly before he crept out at nightfall to find a more secure hiding place in the woods.

But Patton didn't know that he was hiding there in the woods, waiting to be rescued, and so the headlong push of the tanks slowed while they waited for the slower moving supply trucks to catch up. And Bud sat in his hole and waited. One night he stole into a nearby field and dug up some of last year's turnips that had been left in the ground. They were not good but they were food, and he needed food. But still the tanks loitered in the distance.

He had lost all hope and was preparing to give himself up to the first German he saw, when the tanks began to move again. In a matter of a few hours they had swept past him and he was able instead to stagger out to greet the first support troops following hard behind the fighting.

That should have been the end of Bud's troubles, but it wasn't. He was rather quickly evacuated to France, but there he was told that he could not go back to England. The rules and regulations were very clear: all returning prisoners of war were to be processed through Fécamp and returned to the United States, not England.

He ranted and raved. He went to see the chaplain. He threatened and cajoled. But it was all no good. The answer still was that he must go back to the United States. So Bud did what any reasoning man in like circumstances would have done: he went AWOL. Ranking officers do not often go AWOL, but Bud did. He simply walked out of the camp and hitched a ride to Le Havre.

It didn't last. The port authorities picked him up immediately and returned him to Fécamp. He was lectured severely, but he was not punished. And he was not guarded.

That was a mistake on the part of the authorities, for Bud didn't let his shirt-tail touch him until he went AWOL again. This time he planned a bit better and headed for Paris. Once there he located friendly officers who looked the other way when he boarded a C-47 headed for London.

So the long-delayed wedding was performed and he had the audacity to take the leave that had been granted so many months before. Then he turned himself in to the authorities at his old station.

Topper

His name was Forbes. We called him Topper. Top for short.

Topper gave every evidence of being an easy-going Southern boy who would not know how to make his way through Europe and would not try it even if given the chance. He spoke no foreign languages -- even the little bit of German that he had picked up was so tinged with his drawl that no one was ever going to be fooled into thinking him anything but American. He looked American. He sounded American. He even resented being called a Yankee because it implied to his mind that he was something other than a deep-south American.

But looks and language are not necessarily the measure of a man. For Top's brain was constantly seething with plans to escape. And his plans, contrary to those of most of us, had a lot of thought and logic put into them. The Escape Committee was often hard-put to find the flaws in them although they obviously did contain flaws, for Top came home on the same ship that I did. It was just that the flaws always turned out to be such unexpected things. Like the trip to Switzerland.

While we were in Sagan Top disappeared one day. And it was in the daytime, for he had been present at morning *appell* and at the evening count we were shifting and filling to cover for him, hoping to gain enough time for him to get clear of the area. I never knew how he got out of the compound; at the time I didn't ask, for the less one knows about such things the less one can reveal. But he did get out and we were successful in covering for a full twenty-four hours.

Topper had escaped before. Once he simply walked out the gate behind a detail that was being moved from one compound to another. He didn't get very far that time, but it didn't discourage him. Another time he got out, I don't know just how, and managed to get to a town thirty miles away before the Germans caught up with him. His lack of German tripped him up that time when he tried to get a train timetable from a ticket counter. The ticket agent spoke to him, and he could not answer.

He had escaped before and each time there had been slip-ups that brought him back to the Cooler and eventually back to us in the compound. But this time his plans were so specific that no one could find any reason why he would not be able to make it. Much later I learned that he had got detailed information from a tame goon on the rail schedules, had even got diagrams of the rail yard at Sagan, and knew where the guards would be posted in it.

So he hid in the woods during the day, relying on us to cover for him during *appell*. And when night fell he crept into position in the high grass along the edge of the tracks. He counted the trains as they came and went, waiting for that one train that would give him a chance of getting clear. If he took the wrong one he could end up in Berlin or Hamburg or Bremerhaven. Or anywhere else, for that matter.

And taking the train didn't mean stepping into the comfort of a Pullman coach. If he was to be successful at this thing he would have to hide among the carriages of freight; maybe even "ride the rods", as the hobos of the Depression called it. He would have no opportunity to get food or water along the way. He had to be prepared to survive on the minimum rations for as long as it took for the train to work its way down through the Czech mountains into Austria, through Salzburg and Innsbruck and the Stuben Tunnel past Feldkirch. And from a village there he would have to make his way on foot over the mountains into Switzerland.

It was a demanding course he had set for himself, but luck and good planning were with him. His train came precisely on time and stopped in just the right position to permit him to conceal himself among the cars in that few seconds while all the guards were busy at something else and the train crew were gathered around the little old woman at the station with her pots and kettles of strange brews.

The days and nights became an interminable blur as the train lurched southward. There was the endless shifting of cars at each stop, always giving grounds for worry about having chosen the right car to hide him. What would he do if they disconnected his car and left it sitting in some rail yard? How would he find the right train, even assuming that he managed to stay concealed until the right train came along?

And hunger and thirst were constant companions to the jiggling and shaking of his precarious perch. His stock of food and water were minimal at best; an "iron-ration" of concentrated chocolate and raisins and a liter bottle of water. The food was gone by the time he reached Salzburg and the water was going too rapidly even though he doled it out to himself in terms of drops only.

But his luck held. The train hesitated only for a few minutes in the yards at Innsbruck before it headed out on the hard climb up to the tunnel at Stuben and then uncoiled itself down the mountains toward Feldkirch.

The night was inky black when he slipped from the carriage and scrambled into the ditch, waiting for the train to leave again and for the flurry of officials and rail workers to go back to their warm fires and comfortable chairs. It was a cold and damp ditch, and his muscles were knotted and aching from the days and nights of clinging to his hiding place, but it was almost at his journey's end. Just over the mountains and he would be in Switzerland.

He lay quietly, worrying about getting the right direction when he struck out, hoping that he would be able to elude the border guards, wondering if his crude map was accurate. At last the hustle of the departing train died down, the people all went back into the warm and brightly lighted station, and he was left alone in the darkness. He stared for a long time at the windows of the station, marveling that they were so confident that they did not even bother to pull the black-out curtains.

As his eyes became accustomed to the darkness he began to move slowly and very quietly in the direction of the open country. The town was very small, just a jumble of houses beside the river and the tracks, so it was a very simple matter to quickly disappear into the scattering of trees along the riverbank. Once a dog barked somewhere in the smudge of buildings that loomed above him along the embankment, but it was just a questioning sort of bark as if he had dreamed something and was awakened by the dream. Nothing else disturbed his slow progress toward open country and Switzerland.

Once clear of the town, he stopped to drink his fill from the river and to refill his water bottle. And as the grey light came announcing dawn he struck hard uphill in the direction of the border.

And now he travelled in daylight for it was wild country, not likely to have anyone puttering about. And he would be able to see anyone in plenty of time to hide. So he strode on, gaining height quickly as the sun rose higher and higher.

That night he shivered with the cold but kept moving. He felt that he had a better chance of getting past the border guards at night. They were not likely to be on the look-out for an escaped prisoner of war at any time, and certainly not at night. So he pushed on. If his estimates of distance traveled were right he should cross into Switzerland sometime about four in the morning.

With sunrise came a sense of elation. He felt certain that he was in free territory now. All he had to do was keep walking until he found a road, and then he could stop the first vehicle that he saw. He was free! He could go to the American Consulate and send messages home! He could talk to free men again! He was free!

He found a swift-flowing mountain stream and followed it down, knowing that, sooner or later, it had to lead to roads and men and freedom. It led him through a swift succession of joinings with other streams, then spread into a broad, placid river with high banks and roads on either side. He chose the one on the right bank and followed it down for some distance. There was no traffic. He could not even hear the noises of farmers at their morning chores. He was beginning to wonder if he shouldn't back-track and take the other road when he spotted a man moving toward him.

At first glance he had thought it to be a farmer going out to his fields or herds, but then he saw the gun and knew that this was no farmer. But no matter, a Swiss was a Swiss whether he be soldier or farmer. He raised his voice in a shout that made the man look up sharply and motion for him to come down to meet him. Topper broke into a trot, his water bottle slapping awkwardly at his thigh. His mind was filled with the good food he would have today, the soft bed he would sleep in tonight, all the good and lovely things of being in a free country.

Too late he realized that the soldier was German. He had walked into Switzerland and out again without ever knowing it.

So it was back in the cooler again.

Carlyle

In World War I he would have been called shell-shocked. In the Second World War it was called battle fatigue. We simply thought of him as being very nervous. And he was entitled to it.

Sometimes his nervousness brought down the displeasure of the authorities on his head and, incidentally, on the heads of those around him. Like his reaction to the muffled sounds of ferrets under the building. He seemed to be able to hear the slightest sound and could detect a ferret long before anyone else was even vaguely aware of his presence. He would begin pacing back and forth, moving out into the hallway to get more room. And as he paced his footsteps would become louder and louder until he would be stamping his feet directly over the poor ferret's head. More than once we were all threatened with the Cooler because he scared a ferret out of his wits.

Ferrets were guards whose specialty was snooping out the secrets of the prisoners. They rummaged under the buildings, looking for tunnels and eavesdropping on conversations. They crept from rafter to rafter in the attic looking for clandestine radios, escape equipment, or anything else that they might find. By the very nature of their work they developed a shifty eye and furtive gait, so that they were identifiable at a glance although we were not supposed to know the ferrets from the regular guards. But they gave themselves away.

Carlyle's nervousness came of seven months in France, moving from one hiding place to another constantly in order to stay ahead of the Nazis. He was in the hands of the Underground, of course, but his hiding places were sometimes precarious at very best. He spent a week holed up in the attic of the building which housed the Gestapo officers in one town. In another he lived for days in the tiny storeroom next to the room of a German officer.

That was the place where he learned to control a sneeze. We found out about it because, to him, a sneeze was an excruciating experience that involved enormous facial contortions, a racking of the body that was painful to witness, and an ending that was all anticlimax. For the sneeze simply died unborn. The whole process left him limp, but he did not make a sound.

And the lack of sound was the key to the whole performance. During those days and nights when he lay huddled in the dark with just the thickness of a plaster wall between him and the German officer's bed, he had suffered with a head cold and had been alternately chilled and fevered. His body demanded that he give free rein to the sneezes and coughs, but his mind would not. Just one little sniffle and his secret would be out and he would be on his way to some jail. So he stifled the urge and won.

But he didn't win out over that jail. The *Gestapo* came on the morning that he was to go down to the beach to be ferried through the fog in a rowboat to some unknown fishing boat. He had been betrayed. He and a dozen others who never made it to that trawler.

He had been in hiding so long that all evidence of his American citizenship had been replaced with articles showing him to be French. His uniform, of course, was long ago replaced with civilian clothing. His dog tags had been thrown away and he carried a forged work permit. With that kind of evidence against him it is a wonder that they didn't just shoot him on the spot.

Instead they put him in the *bastille* at Lille. It was a grim place, reserved mostly for the more dangerous and more important prisoners. It was considered to be escape-proof.

And it was. Except for the raid by a Mosquito bomber. One night after he had been there for weeks of grilling and mental torture, a single bomber came in low across the fields and skipped a bomb into the wall of the prison. It exploded a few yards from where Carlyle sat in his cell. So I suppose that shell-shocked would be a good description of his nervousness, after all.

While that one bomb didn't get him free of the prison, it did seem to weaken the determination of the Germans to make him admit to being a resistance fighter. Soon after the incident they transferred him, without explanation, to the interrogation center at *Dulag* and, eventually, to Sagan.

But back to the story of his torment of the ferrets. Soon after the Allied invasion of France we were besieged by ferrets. They crept under the building during the night and lay hidden the next day, hoping to overhear a conversation that might be revealing. They searched our meager belongings while we were out for *appell*. They pulled unannounced searches. They were trying to find the radios that they knew we had.

There had been no real secret about the radios from the beginning. It was just that they couldn't find them when they pulled a search. But we had been a little too blatant about our information when the landing was taking place. We told the German guards before the official radio announced it! And that didn't sit too well with some of their higher authorities. They were determined now to find the radios and to punish the offenders.

Carlyle was in a fever of running back and forth along the hallway and into other rooms while all this was going on. He couldn't sit still while a ferret was near. His constant fidgeting set some of us plotting one day, planning ways to drive the ferrets around the bend without getting into trouble ourselves. I think it was Jake who first got the idea, but soon everyone was taking turns at going for walks around the compound so that we could talk without being overheard. In a matter of hours our plans began to shape up into a concerted effort to be purposely careless and noisy, particularly when it would most discomfit the ferrets.

So we set about the task. First there was the case of the unbalanced locker. At least we insisted to the *feldwebel* that it had been tipsy from the very start. It was a heavy wooden locker -- a double locker, in fact -- which was intended for the storage of clothing and equipment, and it could be over-balanced only with great difficulty. But we marshalled enough manpower to be able to pick it up and move it silently. When Carlyle heard a ferret moving around under the building we generated a covering noise -- I think it was a wrestling match that time -- and, while he pinpointed the location of the ferret, we picked the locker up and moved it until it was directly over the man. Then we pushed it over so that it slammed down on the floor just inches above his head. The racket must have been enough to deafen him. Then we picked it up and "accidentally" dropped it again.

That last was too much for the poor man. He let out a howl that could have been heard in Berlin and came clawing his way out from under the building. When the *feldwebel* came in to investigate we insisted that it had all been a terrible accident and we were very sorry that the poor ferret had hurt his head getting out. He knew that we were guilty, but he couldn't shake our story so he finally let us off with a threat to send us to the Cooler next time.

A few days later the same ferret climbed into the attic during one of the daylight searches. There were half a dozen other Germans in the immediate area, so it took a bit of doing to steal the ladder but we did it. While Bob and A Louie started a loud argument and the rest of us crowded in to make it look like trouble might start at any moment -- while the guards were distracted with our angry shouting -- Jake picked up the ladder and walked to the other end of the hallway with it. He put it into the latrine and then returned to the still raging argument. Gradually we let it die and the searchers finished their task and moved on to the next room.

It was only when all the rooms had been searched and the ferret had thoroughly sifted the dust in the attic that anybody missed the ladder. The other guards had moved on to the next building when the ferret popped his face down through the crawl-hole and demanded to know where his ladder was. We insisted that the others must have taken it with them, and we made no move to help the fellow down from his dusty perch. He blustered and threatened, but finally he lowered himself as far as he could through the opening and then fell the rest of the way.

Disposal of the ladder could have been a problem. Having stolen it, we didn't want to turn it back to the goons again. And we couldn't leave it there in the latrine to be found by them later. In the end it served a good purpose, however. It was split into kindling wood and parcelled out to several rooms where it was the fuel that cooked that night's supper.

I've often wondered how the ferret explained the disappearance of the ladder.

Carlyle's specialty came to be a sort of scraping noise that drove the ferrets to a frenzy of searching. When he detected one in the building he would go to the concrete slab on which the stove sat and would begin to make scraping and scratching noises along the edges of it. Apparently this sound carried very well in the space beneath the building and the ferrets were ever mindful of the fact that the tunnels of the year before had been dug under these slabs.

After a minute or two of scraping, when the ferret had had time to zero in on the sound, Carlyle would move to the room across the hall and repeat the performance. Soon the building would be swarming with goons, prying into all the corners, probing around the slabs, checking for telltale dirt where there should be none. He was persuaded to stop this game of baiting the ferrets only when a tunnel was actually under construction in another building. But, in the meantime, he gave them fits.

B Louie

In our combine we had two men named Louie. This presented a conversational difficulty for no one ever knew which one we were talking to. The old army standby of using last names just didn't seem appropriate under the circumstances, so we resolved it by alphabetizing the two names. In short order they became A Louie and B Louie, the precedence having been decided on the basis of physical size. A Louie was a loose-limbed, big man of six feet while B Louie was small and wiry, with the flint-hard body of a circus athlete.

It was B Louie who first mentioned the nocturnal singing. It had begun in the darkness, faintly, distantly. And it had faded away as I came awake enough to wonder who and where it was coming from. I had convinced myself that it was only a dream and had gone back to sleep.

Next morning over our breakfast coffee B Louie wanted to know if anyone else had been awakened by the singing in the night. Of course we all had, and we set to speculating about where it was coming from. Most of us were inclined to think that it was one of the goons playing records again in the *vorlager*. They had done that before, played records loudly in their quarters so that we could hear the strains of music drifting out on the still air. But they had never done it at night before.

And we wondered about the music itself. I had

not really identified the music except to know that it was a human voice apparently unaccompanied. But others said that it was a woman singing and that the music seemed to be 'Indian Lovesong'.

Other things soon absorbed our attention and we forgot the incident. But the singing repeated itself a few nights later. This time it was clearly distinguishable as 'Indian Lovesong' sung in a high, clear soprano. Next morning we commented on it, and we wondered about it, and then we put it out of our minds as being one of those things we would probably never get an explanation for.

But the music would not go away. It came again and again in the still hours of the morning, always the same voice and same song, just a wisp of sound floating in the darkness. And we began to question other people, people who lived in other rooms of the barracks or in other barracks entirely, question them to learn if they too were being awakened by the song. It seemed very strange, but only the twelve of us in that one room ever heard it.

And so, finally, we faced the fact that it was not coming from the *vorlager*, that it had to be one of us. But who? And how did he produce that high soprano voice? At one time or another we each were accused by the others of having perpetrated the joke, and each accusation was in turn withdrawn as it became obvious that our deep masculine voices would not have been capable of producing that sound. We settled, finally, with the idea that Jake had somehow managed it. It just had to have been Jake because he was such a practical joker.

With the realization that it was a practical joke the music stopped. We were no longer awakened in the night by that haunting, lyric voice. And we almost wished it could come back, for it added a spice to our otherwise dull lives.

It was months later in the midst of the Nuremburg bomb raids that the truth finally came out. Through the rattle of ack-ack and the booming of the bomb explosions in the town, suddenly I heard the strains again of the 'Indian Lovesong'. And Jake was nowhere near.

A new drop of chandelier flares blazed over our heads, shedding a cold white light on the trenches and the huddled forms in them. There with a blanket folded over his head and a cherubic smile on his face sat B Louie singing. Not just singing, but singing in that high pure soprano voice that seemed to come from nowhere and everywhere. I would not have believed him capable of it but there it was. I was seeing his lips move as they formed the words. B Louie was our soprano.

A restored B-17 of the Confederate Air Force. Photo by David Rogers.

Goon tower.

Appears to be the front gate at Moosburg.

Barracks interior, possibly at Nurnberg, but it could be at any of the camps.

This may have been made at Sagan. It looks like a baseball game in progress. Baseball was a favorite occupation in the summer of '44 in Sagan.

On the move. Interior of a box car. (Stamped "Box Car Interior" on back)

Wash house, probably at Nurnberg. It was stripped of its walls for use as fuel.

Contraband

He came to me one morning soon after *appell*, joining me as I walked along the path from the assembly field to the barracks. He wore his overcoat against the slight chill of the morning and I thought at the time that it was odd, for he was the man who had spent the past summer wearing the least possible clothing. But now that autumn had come and the air had a bit of a snap to it, he was apparently reversing his form.

I didn't know him well. I had seen him at the cookhouse and at the library. He may even have attended some of my classes, I really don't know. I recognized him on sight, knew that his name was Paul, that he played baseball in nothing more than a breechclout, and that was about all I knew about him. Certainly we were not on such intimate terms as to warrant this sudden show of friendliness.

Not that I objected to it. I was always interested in developing new friends. And, too, I had learned very early on that one does not question too quickly the actions of others. There are times when the things that look innocent enough on the surface are really being done to cover something else, something that the goons should not know about or even see.

We chatted lightly of inconsequential things as we made our way past the other buildings to the far corner of the compound where my barracks was. I thought it odd that he passed his own building with no more comment than the fact that he lived there. But then it was becoming increasingly obvious that his was not a casual visit. I kept wondering what sort of escape plan was being worked out that required him to be seen in the open like this, for he had made it a point to say good-morning to the ferret we passed along the way and he seemed to want to be seen by the *feldwebel* and the *hauptman* as they left the compound.

But I didn't ask. If one doesn't know about it one can't give it away by accident.

As we entered the barracks his attitude of casualness dropped almost audibly. Like a pair of muddy overshoes, he left his friendly conversation at the door.

"Quickly! Not too many people should know about this. Which room do you live in?"

I pointed the way and he hurried in, glancing back down the hall to be sure he wasn't being observed by a ferret. Then he opened his overcoat and handed me a small package. It was tightly sealed in brown paper and was about as big as a couple of packs of cigarettes.

"Keep it until I come back for it. And good luck." He threw an appraising glance at Jake and Sam, who had come in just then, and shook his head silently, warning them that this was not something to be questioned or talked about. Then he buttoned up his coat and was gone.

I took the little package and, not knowing what else to do with it, put it in among the socks and cigarettes in the box under my bed. If it was, as I suspected, contraband parts for a radio, I would have to find a better spot for it. But for now it would have to wait. The others were coming back in from *appell* and I didn't want to involve them with knowledge of this thing that could be so dangerous.

And dangerous it could be. There had been radios operating in the camp for some time. This was obvious for we got the latest BBC news read to us each day although the only source for information was supposed to be the official German radio reports which were copied down in the *vorlager* and circulated to us by the goons. The Germans suspected that we might be building radios somehow and they ran random searches to try to catch us at it. And that is where the danger lay. If I should be caught with parts for a radio the very least I could expect would be a long stretch in the Cooler. And there was always the possibility that they would go back to the barbarity of the year before when some escapees had been summarily shot.

So I puzzled over the problem through breakfast and far into the morning, trying to think of a good place to hide the little brown paper package. But no matter how many places I thought of they all had their drawbacks. Either they were too risky in themselves of they would involve someone else in case the barracks was searched. In the end I simply put the package under my own packs of cigarettes and hoped it would go unnoticed.

It must have been a good decision, for the package survived three full-scale searches of the barracks and I have no idea how many surreptitious checks by the ferrets. If they saw it at all they did not question its being there among my socks and drawing pencils and cigarettes.

But I must say that I was not comfortable about it. Each time that a search was announced and we were ordered out of the building, I had that sinking feeling that this time I was going to be found out. It was very hard to turn my back and walk away, knowing that the little brown package was lying there like a ticking time bomb. But to do anything else was to give the whole thing away. If I didn't walk away, and do it nonchalantly too, they would know that something was amiss and would search until they found it. I suffered unbelievable torments of mind during each of those searches but somehow I stuck it out.

Six weeks after he had originally given me the package I happened to meet Paul on the steps at the cookhouse. We exchanged a few pleasantries and had actually started on our separate ways when he turned and called to me. He trotted the few steps it took to bring him up with me and then fell into step as we headed back toward my barracks.

We walked in silence until we came to the fire pool. To anyone observing us we would have looked very commonplace indeed, two men carrying their soup ration for the day back to their own rooms. But inside I was seething with a need to know what he had on his mind. Would he ask for the package back? Would he give me instructions on what to do with it? What did he want me to do? But I didn't ask. We approached the open space around the fire pool in dead silence.

"The package. Give it to George," he said. "He knows what to do with it." And with that he angled off across the compound, taking a circuitous path back to his own barracks.

I got the package out as soon as I could without involving anyone else. I had to wait an hour or two to find a time when no one was around who would ask too many questions, but as soon as I could I got it out and slid it down deep into my coat pocket. Then I hurried off to find George.

It wasn't hard to find him. He lived in the little room at the end of the barracks, the little cubicle that he and Bud shared as the two senior officers in the barracks. I rapped on the door and went in to find him sitting alone at the table, working on his record of food parcel distribution. I laid the package on the table.

"Paul said you needed this," I said, trying to sound less relieved than I felt.

"Yeah. Sure. I sure do." He didn't even look up. He didn't even glance at the package where it lay on the corner of the table. I hurried out, fearful that he might change his mind and tell me to keep it.

Soon after that there was a sudden increase in the amount of information circulating in the barracks, information that could come only from the BBC news broadcasts. If there had ever been any doubt in my mind it was resolved now: I had been concealing at least part of a radio receiver.

The Padre

He was a simple man who would have preferred to be called just Chaplain Allwin. Or, better still, James. But tradition holds that all chaplains in the British army are called Padre, so Padre it was. Padre with a short A. A holdover, no doubt, from the days when Phillip of Spain was the husband of the Queen.

At first he came only on Sunday, escorted through the *vorlager* by a solitary goon who stood, impassive and unblinking, at the back of the room during the whole of Protestant church service. Then he was allowed to add Wednesday afternoon visits to his schedule and the constant company of the goon was discontinued. He was escorted through the gate and then left on his own. Finally he was moved into our compound permanently.

Traces of Cornwall still lingered in his speech and sometimes we found it difficult to follow his meaning through the translations: that is, Cornish to English to American. It is true that we were speaking the same language but, at times, it was hard to believe it. Especially when reading from the King James version of the Bible he would so far forget himself as to lapse into his native accent, giving us what was more nearly the language of King James' time than we had ever heard before. And I must say that the lovely old poetry of the Psalms is not hurt by the accent of such a voice.

He was a small wiry man with hands too big for his wrists. But those hands which were so awkward when they held a book were precision instruments when they held a baseball bat. Up until he moved into our compound he had never seen a game of baseball and was not even sure that it could be considered the pastime of civilized men. The long tedious days of the summer changed all that, however, for some of the men seemed to spend all the daylight hours either playing the game or practicing by bouncing baseballs off the side of the barracks. Perhaps in self-defense against the constant blam-blam of baseballs against the wall, or through a genuine desire to learn more about the game, the Padre began a serious study of it.

His first time at bat proved the value of his study. He took the first pitch and put it squarely between two outfielders, causing them both to run for it with the result that neither caught it. Time after time he would do that, placing the ball at just the right spot to give himself the advantage. He was quickly added as a permanent player on one of the league teams and that team surged ahead of all the others in intramural play.

And he worked on bunting. This was something that was outside his experience entirely, but he took to it with a zest that was characteristic of his approach to everything. He studied the possibilities and tried to put just enough spin on the ball to drop it dead in the dust half way to the pitcher's mound. And as often as not he succeeded.

But the Padre's baseball career came to a sudden halt in September and with it went the entire scheme of intramural play. It all came about because of the visit of a German inspector, an *oberstleutnant* whose sole aim in life seemed to be to make life miserable for us and for the more reasonable of our guards as well. The Padre was practicing his line drives, using the space between the barracks as a field, when the *oberstleutnant* was driven into the compound. He didn't see the car, couldn't see the car because of the buildings, but that didn't make any difference in the final outcome. As the car moved slowly and sedately down the open road through the center of the camp the Padre hit a smashing drive across the road. The two met with predictable results: we lost our baseballs for the rest of the season and the Padre got three days in the Cooler.

But I would love to have seen the pandemonium in that car at the moment of impact. They must have thought that they had been hit by a hand grenade for the canvas-topped doors flew open and the *oberstleutnant* and his entire crew of goons came tumbling out into the dirt. I think that it was the insult to his dignity that cost us the baseballs.

Baiting the Goons

Boredom was a constant problem for us all. We were officers and, under the German understanding of that status, it was unthinkable that we should be expected to work even though we were prisoners. Even if we had volunteered to work at some non-war task our offer would have been rebuffed for the Germans clung to the Prussian concept of an officer as one who is above all work. Physical work, that is. Brain power and sword scars were much respected.

It was this German respect for the officer caste, coupled with our own boredom, which gave rise to one of the more successful of our agitation efforts. Having nothing else to occupy his mind at the moment, someone thought up the idea of demanding enlisted men to serve as orderlies -- batmen, as the British called them. It was such a ludicrous idea, that we be furnished what amounted to servants in our prison. It was so ludicrous that it just might work. We might be able to get some of the enlisted men out of the work details of their camps, get them assigned to us as batmen where they really would not have any more responsibility to work than the rest of us.

So the idea was brought before the Senior Allied Officer where it was hotly debated for several days before it gained his approval. But, once approved, the plan was put into effect posthaste. The word was passed to the other compounds and the big push was on.

The SAO made a big thing of our officer status and pointed out to the *Kommandant* how degrading it was that we, officers and gentlemen in the best military tradition, had no batmen to care for our clothing or to prepare our meals. Indeed, we were forced to the untenable state of becoming mere cooks – *Kuchen-chef* he called it, using his best *Nord Deutch* accent to emphasize the enormity of the injustice that was being done to us.

And the senior officers of the other compounds picked up the theme and played it to a crescendo. The Senior British Officer was particularly persuasive, waggling his enormous moustache up and down as he bemoaned the difficulties of keeping oneself in proper form without the ministrations of a good 'Man'. The whole effort lasted some eight days before the *Kommandant* gave in and ordered the transfer of the enlisted men from the camps at Vienna. We did not get them in the numbers we had been demanding, but we had won anyway.

Once they arrived in Sagan the enlisted men were scattered among the several barracks so as to give the appearance that they were being used as servants. But in reality it was only a ruse to get them out of the work details that had been their existence. And their coming gave us news, in many cases, of friends and crew members from whom we had been separated at *Dulag*.

* * *

Boredom. The lack of any constructive work gave rise to both the best and the worst in efforts to outwit the Germans. Outwit them, harass them, or simply to cause them inconvenience. One of our efforts involved the establishment of an escape language school. Our intention was, and our efforts were directed toward, teaching a man to speak a European language well enough to pass as a European in case he escaped. It was not enough that he learn French or Spanish or Polish -- he must speak the language with the specific accent of a particular region. He must seem to be from Arles or Barcelona or Poznan.

And some bright soul, probably without sanction or knowledge of that august institution, named it the Extension Language Institute of the University of London. This gave us a cover for our real intentions and made us look like good little officer-schoolboys eager to increase our general knowledge by studying a foreign language. And it was such a good cover that the Germans never suspected what we were up to. The *hauptman* seriously considered joining one of our classes in order to improve his French!

* * *

One of the less effective harassing techniques involved drawing pictures of the goon towers and their occupants. This all began as a way of distracting the attention of a goon one day while messages were being flashed between compounds. While my friends inside the barracks used the old Boy Scout thing of transmitting Morse code with mirror flashes, I sat on the steps ostentatiously drawing a picture of the goon box and the goon.

It got his attention, alright, but not in the way we had hoped. We had intended him to be flattered by the fact that he was being portrayed at his martial best, erect and alert at his post. He was only casually interested, however, inspecting the drawing now and then with his binoculars but, for the most part, ignoring my activity. I was frantic that he would spot the mirror flashes and bring our news service to a halt, but if he saw them at all he only thought they were the normal result of someone shaving in the sunshine.

I had failed so completely to get his undivided attention that those of us who were assigned to such artistic tasks decided to change our technique. Instead of trying to appeal to their vanity we began to attack it. We would draw caricatures calculated to insult them.

After a few minutes of drawing there was always the command from the goon box to hold it up for inspection. Then the goon would study it intently through his binoculars, grumbling all the time that we were not holding it still. After a few seconds of scrutiny he would usually lay the glasses down and go back to staring impassively out over the compound. It was only when the drawing was finished and, with it, whatever illicit activity that had been going on inside, that the goon would insist on a really good look at his likeness. And then, more often than not, his reaction was raucous laughter. Somehow we never quite managed to insult them.

* * *

We walked the perimeter rail every day, like automatons. Methodically we would slog through mud and rain to get in our five times around the compound. It was not so much a physical fitness program as a matter of habit. We had begun it in the summer when the weather was fine and we had nothing in particular to do. We continued it on into the autumn because it had become so much a part of our routine that we did not think about it.

"We", in this case, meant Mac and me. We had met by accident during some impromptu sing-along and had found a mutual interest in conversation. So we met each day for five laps around the compound and we talked, not about the mundane things that made up our world, but the great generalities of philosophy and thought.

That is how it was that we saw it happen. We had just rounded the far corner of the baseball field -- really it was the assembly area for head-counts but we played baseball there, too, and called it the baseball field. At that end of the compound the goon towers were more closely spaced, for the forest was there just beyond the wire and seemed to stretch unbroken for miles. Special care was needed here for, if a man ever got over that fence, he could hide out in the forest for days before the Germans could hope to find him. And he might actually get away completely, although I don't know where he would get to in that direction.

We had rounded the corner, sticking close to the perimeter rail, not touching it certainly, but never far from it. This had a double purpose; it insured that we got the maximum mileage from our walk, and it kept the goons in the towers on their toes. We were deep in some discussion that had been suggested during the previous day, and we had both had time to think about it and to marshal our arguments, but they were blown to bits by the chatter of a machine gun. We stood rooted to the spot while our minds said run. And we stared open-mouthed as the echoes died away.

There, directly ahead of us, a human form hung on the wire and slowly, slowly crumpled until it was suspended inert like a sack of meal. There was a ghastly silence that seemed to go on forever, then the shout from the goon tower of "*alles innen.*" We scuttled into the nearest building and peered fearfully out of the door.

He was not one of the men from our compound. What we had seen had taken place across the wire in the South Compound. But we felt an immense sense of loss that any man had died in such circumstances. While we watched, two men were allowed to go to the wire and take the limp form down and carry it away.

Much later I learned the story behind his foolhardy act. He was one of those British airmen who were taken fairly early in the war and he had sweated out the many escape attempts that always seemed to have such promise but somehow always came a cropper. He dug tunnels. He sewed himself into what approximated a water-tight suit and tried to escape inside a honey wagon. He stowed away on the food delivery wagon. But always he was found out before he could get away.

When the escape attempt that almost worked -- the tunnel that got ninety or so men outside the wire -- when that escape was foiled he was standing in line to enter the tunnel. He was caught and clapped into the Cooler without ever having left his own barracks. He was probably saved from being shot then by the fact that he had not actually entered the tunnel, he was only waiting his turn.

That attempt cost a lot of lives. The figures I have heard over the years have varied, but it seems to be somewhere between forty and fifty men who were executed. The rest were held in solitary for varying lengths of time and then finally returned to the compounds.

He brooded about the failure while he was in the Cooler and he brooded about it when he was returned to the compound. It had seemed so perfect at the time and had been so beautifully executed, but where did they go wrong? What could they do the next time to make it work? He turned these things over and over in his mind, going over details with anyone who would listen, trying to find the answer. And trying to find the perfect escape.

His friends tried to distract him, but he persisted in hatching one plot after another. The Escape Committee invariably turned him down, because his plans had now begun to suffer from wishful thinking. He was no longer capable of evaluating the risks.

One of his plans was simply to wait until a certain guard was in the goon tower and then to climb the fence. He felt sure that the guard would hesitate to fire, and that he could go over the top and into the woods before the alarm could be sounded. He practiced running, sprinting madly between the barracks buildings. He timed himself over the thirty yards that he estimated as the distance from the wire to the woods.

And the Escape Committee turned him down

again. They turned him down and they set others to watch him for fear that he would go out and try it anyway. They recognized his desperation, and they hoped to save him from himself.

For months now their constant watch had seemed to work. He had finally settled into a routine of sorts that permitted very little energy to be devoted to escape plans. He seemed at last to have come to an acceptance of his fate.

And then it happened. One moment he had been pounding out tin cans to be used in making cooking pots and the next moment he was striding toward the wire. And Mac and I watched in horror as he folded and sagged over the topmost strands, reaching toward the second fence, the woods, and freedom.

His freedom was absolute.

We did not talk while we watched. We did not discuss the gory scene even when we went back to our own barracks. Or at least I didn't. Mac lived in another building and may have told his roommates, I don't know. But I was too shaken to talk to anyone about it. Of course the order for everyone to go inside in the middle of the day had put the whole camp to buzzing, and the news of the shooting traveled like wild-fire, being shouted from window to window. But I lay on my bunk with my face to the wall and shed bitter tears for a man I had never met, for a man I had seen only once as he tried for freedom.

* * *

It is funny how the mind plays tricks on us, suppressing details of events that could have been dangerous at the time. Or maybe it is that we play tricks on our minds, ordering a self-preserving forgetfulness that then can not be reversed. Whatever the sequence, the logic of the thing, the fact is that details of an event can be wiped clean from the memory while the event itself remains as vibrant as if it had just occurred.

So it is with our theft of the electrical wire. I

have absolutely no idea what we did with it, but I can still feel the weight of it in the crook of my arm, the almost overpowering urge to break into a run before any of the goons missed it, and the panicky feeling that at any moment the guard in the tower would spot the unwieldy lump under my folded coat.

It was a spur-of-the-moment sort of thing. We were on the last lap around the compound for the day and our conversation had degenerated into a series of little more than grunts and growls. The June sun was beginning to warm up what had started as a miserable day of drizzle and fog.

"Gettin' too hot for a coat."

"Umm?"

"Too hot."

"Uh-huh."

We took our coats off and strolled along with the sun warm on our backs as we approached the double trip-wire that marked the perimeter track between the fence and the site of the new theater building. (It was called a theater although its primary purpose from the goon point of view was as a holding area for the prisoners when they wanted to search our barracks.) On our right was the fence with its goon boxes and concertina wire and beyond that the buildings of the Center Compound. On our left was the framework of the theater and between it and its trip-wire there was a jumble of lumber, saw horses, workmen's tool boxes: all of the things that get scattered around a building site no matter where in the world it is. We walked slowly now, no longer intent on getting in our five rounds, idly watching the work in progress.

If I saw it before he spoke, it hadn't registered as anything more than part of the clutter inside the trip-wire. And certainly I hadn't thought of taking it. But there it lay twenty feet ahead and just inside the forbidden zone — one could easily bend down and scoop it up without missing a step -- a neat coil of insulated electric wire. We had no earthly use for it but it belonged to the German *Reich*.

"Let's steal it." Mac muttered the words under his breath although no one was near enough to have heard or understood even if he had said it aloud. His tone conveyed total seriousness rather than the small-boy bravado one might have expected of such a senseless project. I glanced at his face and saw the same total seriousness there.

As we came abreast of the coil of wire Mac suddenly burst into loud and raucous laughter and swung at me in mock anger. It was the sort of horseplay that kids engage in everywhere. I ducked from the blow and lost my balance, almost going over the trip-wire into the building area. When my left hand came away from the ground I had the coil of wire.

It was heavy, bulky—a cumbersome thing to try to hide. How was I to carry the thing away without being caught? Panic welled up inside me at the thought of what I had done. For a moment I stood in mental nakedness, the very wood of the surrounding goon boxes seeming to accuse me. I felt as if I were being watched by every workman and every ferret within the compound. I fought to choke back the panic.

There was no hue and cry from the workmen. The goons in their boxes continued their staring out into space. The world went on as if I did not have twenty pounds of wire dangling from my hand. Slowly—ever so slowly it seemed to me — I conquered my panic, draped my coat over the wire and hugged it to me.

Those last hundred yards or so to the barracks seemed to take forever. We kept up a steady stream of chatter, bumping and poking one another the way kids do. But inside we were so tensed up that we would have bolted at the slightest motion by a goon.

As I said, I don't remember what we did with the wire — hid it away somewhere, I suppose, and eventually delivered it to the Escape Committee for whatever use they might make of it. But that detail of the theft is wiped clean in my mind. I have no idea what we did with it, but I can still feel the urgency of its weight in my hand.

Hasenfalle

Sam was the first to see it, and everyone thought he was joking when he told us about it. It was simply unthinkable that a rabbit would have come through the fences in the glare of the floodlights to nose about among the anemic peppers and squashes that constituted our garden. But next morning there were the unmistakable tracks in the dust and a few nibbled leaves to attest to the fact. As he closed the wooden shutters over the windows for lock-up for the night Sam had caught a glimpse of the rabbit and had called the rest of us to look. But it was gone in the shadows before the words were out of his mouth.

We watched each evening after that to see if we could get another look, but lock-up time usually came before the rabbit did. His tracks were evident on most mornings and a few more leaves would have been nibbled, but we were not successful in getting a look at him. He seemed to have an uncanny sense of timing, coming into our garden just after the shutters were closed and departing again before the guard dogs were led into the compound.

At first we were just curious and a bit protective of our pitiful garden plants, not wanting to hurt the rabbit but not wanting him to destroy anything either. We tried leaving the shutters open just a crack so that we could peek out now and then and maybe scare him away, but that didn't work. The patrolling goon always spotted the open shutter and slammed it shut and bolted it from the outside. Even when we turned the light out he spotted it, so we gave that up for fear of jeopardizing other activities. If we pushed it too far the goons would get suspicious and pull a full-scale search of the block, and probably all the other blocks in that end of the compound. There was just no knowing what might be uncovered by such a search. Our garden really wasn't worth the risk.

The slow nibbling away of our garden continued although it was difficult to understand why the rabbit would prefer those wilted and sickly plants to the vigorous grasses of the woods across the fence. And Sam worked at schemes to catch him. He tried several kinds of snares, but gave up on each one before it was finished because it became obvious that it would not work. And there was also the problem of getting permission to set a snare. The goons patrolled the area at night with guard dogs and they took a very dim view of anything that might conceivably distract or endanger their dogs. So even if he found a workable scheme, Sam faced the prospect of having to justify its use and assure the Germans that it represented no danger to them or to their dogs.

His final solution involved using our coal-box. It was a small wooden box, of very solid construction, intended to hold the fuel for our stove. On those rare occasions when we got coal it was the measure of what constituted a week's ration. But that too was a fiction, for there was no way that so little coal could be stretched to cover a week.

Be that as it may, Sam carefully stacked our tiny

stock of coal briquettes and our hand-dug pine stumps in the corner behind the stove and used the box to fashion a trap. He carefully carved a bit of pine stump to form a prop and trigger arrangement that could be used to hold up one end of the box. The trigger, which projected inside the box, could be baited with something to entice the rabbit inside. And once he touched the trigger the prop would fall and the whole box would come slamming down around him, leaving him unhurt but pinned inside. Sam tested it over and over, using a thin sliver of wood to reach inside and trip the trigger. It worked with the slightest touch, yet stood up ruggedly to contact outside the box.

So all that was left was to get permission to use it. His efforts through the normal channels met total indifference on the part of the underlings who handled such things in the *vorlager*, but fate took a hand. Sam sat in the afternoon sun, brooding over what he took to be his failure to get permission for its use, setting up the trap, tripping it, and then setting it up again, when the *feldwebel* came striding past. He paused, looked intently at the trap, and then started on. But he changed his mind and came back.

"How is it said in English, this thing, this *hasenfalle*?" Perhaps he had seen the request for permission to use it. Or perhaps he had trapped rabbits himself when he was a boy, using such a box and trigger. Certainly his English was good enough that only a word like "rabbit trap" would have required translating. But he gave the impression that this was his first knowledge of what we had come to call Operation Br'er Rabbit.

"Rabbit trap," Sam told him, carefully balancing the box again on its prop and tripping the trigger with just the tiniest of touches. "See the tracks there. And those gnawed leaves. That rabbit is ruining our garden."

"And do you have permission to use it? Is it approved by *der hauptman*?"

"No. Not yet. It went to the vorlager day before yesterday but nothing has come back yet. If they don't hurry up there is not going to be anything left of this garden. Not that it is much as it is, but it is all we have." Sam was genuinely aggrieved that the petty bureaucrats were dawdling over his request while the rabbit grew fat.

The *feldwebel*, looking thoughtful, bent over to carefully inspect the trap, running his fingers over the smooth wood of the prop and trigger mechanisms and checking it to see if any modifications had been made to the coal box. When he had satisfied himself he straightened up and smiled.

"What will you use to call the rabbit? What food? How is it you say -- what bait?" The *feldwebel* clearly seemed interested in the project.

"Kohlrabi leaves, I guess. That is about all we have to attract him."

"No, no! Try to find something sweeter. Rabbits will not eat kohlrabi if there is anything else. Try a bit of potato or a carrot top if you have it. That will tempt him. No, kohlrabi leaves will never catch him." And the *feldwebel* went on his way then, whistling to himself and seeming to give no further thought to the rabbit. But that afternoon at *appell* Sam got permission to set up his trap. It had to be set before the evening lock-up and it couldn't be checked until after morning roll call, but at least he had permission.

That first night the trap was tripped by a guard who stumbled over it in the dark. We heard the thump as he hit it with his foot and the startled woof of his dog as the box fell. There was a muttering of black oaths, and then total silence as the man and the dog went their way. But we could not get out to reset the trap until the next morning. The rabbit had probably come and gone by then anyway.

Then there were a couple of nights when the baited trap sat untouched through a gentle drizzle. Apparently the rabbit did not venture out in the dampness, at least not so far as to raid our garden.

We talked about the rabbit, about what we would do when Sam caught it. We were unanimous that we should eat it but were, for the most part, uncertain about how to cook it. In the long run the cooking of it would be Oscar's problem but we debated it anyway. And we considered the prospects for using the trap to catch birds but quickly gave up the idea, realizing that the few pigeons we saw above the tree tops never seemed to venture into the compound. Later in Nuremburg we would see thousands of pigeons around us when we no longer had the materials for trap making, but here there seemed to be very few and they were very wary.

Then came the night when we heard the trap sprung. We had waited expectantly during that twilight time when the rabbit would ordinarily have been feeding, and we had waited in vain. There had been no sound from the garden and, one by one, we had finally dropped off to sleep. We were awakened by the thump of the box as it fell and the hiss of a cat caught by surprise.

"That sounded like a cat!" someone whispered in the darkness.

"Couldn't be," someone whispered back. "Cats don't eat carrots. And what would a cat be doing in the compound, anyway?"

"What about a rabbit? What's he doing here?" There was the flare of a match, a cigarette glowed in the dark and the room fell quiet again. We went back to sleep to wait for daylight and a chance to inspect the trap.

When the goons unlocked the buildings and hustled us out for *appell* we fidgeted and fumed while the *hauptman* went through his meticulous count and then repeated it to be sure that he was not missing a man. When he finally had done with it and the *feldwebel* had read all of the day's announcements to us before dismissing us, we broke and ran back through the compound toward our trap. By now it had ceased to be Sam's trap; it had become our trap. Though Sam had done all the work on it we each felt a proprietary interest.

Someone raised the box an inch or two and Sam put his hand under the edge to try to catch the rabbit. Since the box was solid all around he was having to work in the blind, unable to see the animal, only to feel for it under the box. As he worked his arm under, slowly feeling his way from one edge to another, he suddenly jerked upright and yelped in pain.

"That ain't no rabbit," he said, as he dabbed at the blood beginning to trickle from four long scratches across the back of his hand. "It's a cat. And I ain't sure how we are going to get him out without getting clawed some more. No telling what he might do if we just lifted the box off of him!"

"Ever try to eat a cat?" someone ventured.

"No, and I'm not planning to start now! All I want to do is get him out of my trap so I can catch a rabbit!" Sam sounded so disgusted we had to laugh. The thought of eating a cat had not really occurred to any of us before and Sam's explosive reaction to the idea struck us as being hilarious.

In the end we got rid of the cat by tying our clothesline to the box and standing back a safe distance to pull it off of him. As soon as the box was raised high enough to permit him out, he erupted in a flurry of claws, fur, and hisses and disappeared through the fences in the direction of the woods. All we saw was a tawny blur as he raced through the coils of barbed wire and across the cleared space on the other side of the fence, disappearing into the shadows of the woods.

Sam reset the trap each night for weeks after that but the rabbit never came back. Maybe the smell of the cat remained in the box and so discouraged him from foraging in our garden. Or maybe he just lost interest. But the thing we wondered most about was why the cat was there in the first place. Because cats don't eat carrots.

In the desolate camp of Nuremburg we knelt side by side scraping at the bottom of an air-raid trench with our makeshift tools. Sam had worked steadily for an hour or so, silently deepening the trench against the expected raid by the night-bombers. He had not seemed to notice the flutter of the pigeons along the roofs nor even to be aware of those of us who worked beside him. We all were hungry-thin and weak, our strength sapped by the cold, exhaustion, and malnourishment. Sam was in no better condition than any of the rest of us but he had a doggedness that drove him on to finish whatever he started. And he was determined to make the trench a foot deeper.

A pigeon fluttered from a roof and landed on the pile of dirt that we had thrown up from our digging. It cocked its head on one side and looked at us warily as it side-stepped its way up the mound toward some suspected tidbit of a worm. Sam glanced up then and stopped his shoveling for a moment. The pigeon and the man stared at one another across the space of four feet or so before the bird took flight and flew back to his perch. Sam picked up his tin-can shovel again and muttered to himself as much as to anyone else:

"I wonder how that cat would taste now."

V

Evacuation of Sagan

There had been an air of expectation in the camp for days now. First we had heard the clatter of armored vehicles during the night as they were moved eastward, then the faint rumbling of gunfire a few nights later. It was like a thunderstorm in the distance except that it kept up its low muttering all night long. And the next night it grew a bit louder, or we thought it did. And there was that order from the Senior Allied Officer that we should start a fitness program in earnest in case we were forced to march.

Our clandestine radios told us that the Russians were pushing hard toward the west and Berlin. We didn't know exactly how far away they were -- our maps were totally unreliable -- but we knew that we stood between them and Berlin. The sound of their gunfire was a singing in the blood, a rippling, bubbling, happy sound of liberation. To us it was not ominous, not a death-dealing sort of sound: it was beautiful.

We began to try to estimate the distance to the guns by listening to the sound through the ground. It was an old trick we had learned as boys; if you put your ear to a railroad track you can hear a train miles before it comes near you. And after a little practice you can gauge the distance by the intensity of the vibration. We played at that sort of thing when I was a boy. So Top and I would go to opposite ends of the compound, lie face down on the ground, and try to get a good estimate of the distance and direction of the gunfire. Then we would meet and try to work a triangulation to determine how far it really was. Our estimates tended to be wildly erratic, for we had no second source to use as a counter. If only we could get out at night when we could see the flashes on the horizon!

Our guards soon became curious about our peculiar action and began to investigate. Each time that we lay down on the ground a guard would come rushing up and demand that we get up. Once, after I had carefully explained to one goon what I was doing and why, he too lay on the ground listening. And he was fascinated by this new knowledge. He kept me standing in the cold for several minutes while he questioned me about judging the distance, and he wondered aloud how this obvious proximity of the Russians could be squared with the official reports which had them still on the east border of Poland.

The nightly parade of noises grew louder and closer, and the sense of exhilaration mounted with it. Men sewed together packs to carry their few belongings and they trudged endlessly around the perimeter rail. It was no longer a listless plodding for lack of anything better to do; now they walked with a swing to their steps and determination written large on their faces. How little they knew how that determination was to be called into play later.

In a matter of days our radios were telling us that the Russians had crossed the river at Breslau and were besieging the city. The official German newscasts still had them far to the east. We waited breathlessly, knowing that no natural obstacles stood now between us and the liberating army. The Escape Committee met and drew lots to determine the few who could be supported for the days necessary in the tunnel beneath the theater -- this in case we were moved out on short notice. And they collected all of the unpunched cans of food that had been hoarded against a day of possible escape. Everything was spirited into the tunnel and stowed away in readiness for the final days.

And those final days dragged on in what seemed an eternity. The Russians seemed to run out of steam as they slowly absorbed the last pockets of resistance at Breslau. Their headlong push all along the line seemed to waver and come to a halt.

Then all hell broke loose. As January was wearing itself out the entire eastern front in Poland seemed to erupt. The day dawned with a low-hanging sky that looked like old pewter and in the distance there was the usual rumble of cannon. Not loud and insistent, but low and rumbling as if to tell the *Wehrmacht* that the Russians were still there, even if they were not very active. But at mid-morning the rumble suddenly became a din as every available gun was brought into use and aircraft skittered across treetops, firing at anything that looked like a target.

And activity in the *vorlager* erupted, too. Goons scurried in and out and there was much Nazi saluting and hand-shaking as various German officials came and went. We could almost hear the click of heels and the muttered "*Heil, Hitler*!" that went with the salutes.

The rumor spread that we would evacuate and men began to sort their meager belongings and determine what should be left behind and what would be useful to carry. We had our evening meal amid talk of what should be carried and what should be discarded. Most of us favored carrying only the essentials -- food, extra clothing, cigarettes. Very few felt it wise to try to carry out the less useful things. I burned a year's accumulation of sketches rather than burden myself with them.

And, for once, the rumor proved to be true. At midnight we were assembled in a long, straggly column down the center of the compound, the gates were opened and we marched out with our guards flanking us on either side.

There had been snow some days before, but it had melted from the roads and the slush had frozen over so that walking was not bad. And our days and weeks of walking the perimeter rail stood us in good stead. In fact, we were, in many cases, in better condition for the march than our guards were. I can still hear the "*langsam*, langsam" of little Fritz as he struggled to keep up with the column. His short legs flailed the ground furiously and he panted and snorted as he struggled not to be left behind by his captives.

We marched all night and through the morning as the sounds of gunfire became more distant. We rested when it became essential, but we did not waste any time. The German officials seemed to be particularly fearful of lingering where the Russians might catch us up. At last, at noon we stopped and slept. Some slept in the hay of village barns, others in the dairy sheds. I slept soundly on the floor of a kitchen, watched over by a wide-eyed Pole and his wife.

And while we slept the snow came again. It fell silently, in a deep blanket that masked the roads and streams so that everything looked the same. All distinguishing marks were obliterated; only an occasional fence showed where a road might be. And we were brought out into this and set to march again as night fell and the temperature dropped.

Most of that night is a void in my mind, overridden by the intense cold and fatigue. But somewhere along the line, as we moved along a dark track through a forest, there was the sound of an airplane and someone yelled "air-raid!" The whole column, guards and guarded alike, disintegrated into the forest.

My instinctive reaction was to think of escape and to look for ways to carry it off. I had hit the snow where I thought there was a small embankment and found to my delight a neatly concealing bush and snow bank. From my vantage point I could see out onto the road but could not be seen from it. I began to work my way deeper into the snow, intending to stay put when the column moved on.

The minutes dragged by with no return of the airplane and the guards began to round up the prisoners and line them up again on the dimly visible road. I lay very still in my hole, trying not to move when the snow would sift down my collar, trying to ignore the coldness in my feet, wanting to move them about to get the circulation going again but not daring to do it. I got colder and colder, but I did not move.

The column seemed about complete now on the road and the few who had tried to run away into the woods had been stopped and brought back. A few shots had been fired but no one seemed to have been hurt. I clenched my teeth together to keep them from chattering and hoped that the goons would not take a headcount. If only they would move off so that I could get the blood moving again in my cold feet!

They didn't take a headcount. They did something totally unexpected and out of character; they sent guards out into the woods far past my position and brought them sweeping back in toward the column. This tactic flushed several more prisoners who seemed to have had the same idea that I did, but it left me still deep in my hole. I was beginning to feel a surge of elation in spite of the numbing cold, a sense of having put one over on them. I knew and accepted the fact that it would be a long, hard pull to get back to the Russian lines. I was willing to take the risk if they would just move out.

I shifted my position slightly to ease the strain, hoping that the tiny motion would not be noticed.

"Pinggg!" It was a rifle bullet just inches above me. I could not tell where it had come from but it sent me deeper into the hole, adding a trickle of ice water to the sifting of snow down my collar.

I lay very still, hardly breathing, hoping that it was a fluke, a mistaken shot. Maybe he hadn't seen me at all. Maybe he was shooting at something else. I waited.

"*Raus! Raus*!" It was a guard standing on the edge of the road, peering into the trees in my direction.

His rifle was slung on his shoulder so it was not he who had fired at me. But he was being insistent that I "*raus*."

I waited, feeling like a rabbit cornered by the hounds. My feet were beginning to lose their throbbing coldness, tingling instead with blocked circulation.

"*Raus*!" He moved several yards closer to me, coming into the woods a bit uncertainly.

"Pinggg!" Again the bullet whistled past me by a hair's breadth. "*Raus*!" He came closer still.

"Pinggg!" I dared not stand up now. Wherever the goon was, he was certain to drill me now if I moved.

So I waited.

"*Raus*!"

"Pinggg!"

"*Raus*!"

Then he stood looking down at me, stood on the lip of my hiding place with his rifle still slung across his shoulder casually as if he had not thought of using it. I didn't risk finding out if he would. There was that other goon with the gun who had kept up the steady fire that I would have to reckon with.

"*Alles aus*," he said and chuckled. Everybody outside. It was the standard command for a headcount.

* * *

Another memory of that long night haunted me for years. The agony of those last kilometers to Muskau, compounded of the cold and my own stubborn will, is deeply etched in my memory. After the incident with the airplane, our part of the column had become detached from the rest of the vast mass of humanity and we had struggled through the countryside, walking needless miles out of our way, getting colder and weaker as the night and the distance wore on.

When a man could go no further, when his physical strength was exhausted and it was stop or drop, the *feldwebel* would call a halt. He would bring together the worst cases of both prisoners and guards and he would leave them in a barn to rest and to follow on when they were able to march. And the rest of us would move on.

I should have taken one of those rest stops. My feet had lost all sensation. I moved on will power alone. If I ever stopped moving I felt certain that I would never be able to start again. So even at the hourly rests I kept in motion, plodding slowly back and forth along the line of motionless forms.

Most of the night is lost to my memory. It was simply a matter of one cold step after another, following in the wake of the man ahead, trying to avoid the bite of the wind as much as possible, and trying desperately to concentrate on moving forward.

In the last hour or two before dawn, however, my cold-numbed brain seemed to come awake and take notice of the surrounding countryside. We had left the flat ground behind and were winding our way through low, rolling hills. The stark black trunks of the pines of Poland changed to a mixture of firs and deciduous trees with a scattering of undergrowth here and there. The clouds overhead had been shredded by the wind so that wisps of moonlight filtered through now and then, setting lights to sparkling in the crusted snow on the branches.

I suppose it was the moonlight on the snow that set the whole thing off in his mind. I know that I had trouble for some time with lighted windows that were not there, with houses that melted before we reached them. But a handful of snow would douse the ghost-lights and give me back my sanity.

We had set up a buddy system early in the march so that every man watched his companions for signs of weakening. When a man began to waver in his walking, or when he seemed to slump into himself too much, someone would take his arm and, half carrying and half guiding, would help him along until the next rest period.

He had offered his help to me that way. Seeing

me rub snow in my face he had surmised that I was having difficulties and had come to me to buck me up and keep me moving. We had talked as we walked along, the casual sort of talk that is meant to occupy the time and the mind without forming a permanent involvement. He seemed to be in good shape considering the circumstances, trying to keep his mind occupied with the problems of others rather than his own and making a good show of it.

We walked along side-by-side for a kilometer or so, not supporting one another physically yet lending a mutual support that was comforting to us both. The moon glimmered here and there in the forest, giving it an eerie light that flickered and was gone as the wind whipped the clouds across the sky.

"Do you see her there?" He spoke in a hushed voice, half afraid that what he saw was not really there. I saw nothing but was slow to say so.

"There! There! Just beyond those trees. With a lantern. Don't you see her?" He was pointing excitedly into the woods. I still saw nothing, but the vision was obviously getting stronger for him.

"I know who she is! It's Gram, that's who it is! I know it is!" The vision had gone too far. I picked up a fistful of snow to rub into his face to bring him around.

But he was no longer there. He bolted past the staggering guard like a frightened deer and bounded out into the forest. I held my breath, waiting for the shot that would end his vision.

"*Halt! Halt*!" It was a command to the fleeing form as well as to the column. Two goons dropped into a kneeling position, their guns aimed and ready to shoot.

He stopped in a little glade, not because of the cries for him to halt, but because he had lost sight of his vision. The moon had died momentarily and his lights were gone. He stood there, turning first this way and then that as he tried to spot the lantern again. That moment of indecision probably saved his life, for I am sure the goons would have fired if he had kept running.

By now the *feldwebel* had come up at a run to take charge of the situation. He took the whole thing in at a glance and began to issue a stream of orders. The guards lowered their weapons and ceased their shouting at him. One of them took the two prisoners selected by the *feldwebel* and walked out into the woods toward the glade. The *feldwebel* himself began to walk in that direction, talking soothingly as he went.

The stratagem worked. The two prisoners came up to him with no difficulty. He did not try to run away. He seemed completely bewildered by the loss of his vision. But he would not come back to the column. He shook them off each time that they tried to get him moving back toward the rest of us.

Then the *feldwebel* joined the little group. We could not distinguish what was being said, but we could see from the motions that they made that all three were trying to talk him into coming back to us. They were trying to talk him out of his hallucinatory state. And they were not succeeding. He kept backing away, looking about in the trees as if he expected to find her at any moment.

The murmur of the *feldwebel's* voice fell lower and lower as he edged in closer. Then, with a sudden leap, he was on the man and had his arms pinned to his sides.

They brought him back, still babbling and seeing lights, but at least he was no longer in danger of being shot. We put him in the center of the column and four of us kept watch on him.

And we started up the long, cold hill. We had come through low, rolling hills for some distance, but this one was different. We could see the top where the road crested and the tiny slash in the forest wall that was the road itself. It was a long climb, taking all our will power to get us up it, and it was full morning when we reached the top.

We rested there for a few minutes. We all needed the rest, both guards and prisoners. I gingerly took off my shoes and looked at my swollen feet and changed socks, although one pair was no cleaner nor drier than the other.

When the call came to move on we picked ourselves up wearily, flexing muscles to get them working again. Everyone except Higgins, the man who had been brought back from the wood. He lay beside his pack, sleeping the sleep of exhaustion. We got him on his feet and moving again, but it did no good. He would fall asleep in mid-step. We tried carrying him between two of us, but it was slow going and our own weariness made it difficult for two people to act in unison.

We bumbled along this way for an hour, or until the next rest halt was called. When he still could not function after that rest, I gave in to desperation. I handed my pack to the nearest man, threw Higgins over my shoulder, and marched on to Muskau. They told me later that it was a six kilometer march and that I carried him all the way, refusing all offers of help. I don't remember it. My next recollection is of the street in Muskau and the hot tea someone was pouring down my throat.

* * *

We slept that night in a pottery factory. Or, rather, that day and night, for I went to sleep immediately after we got inside and I slept until the following morning. The factory was warm and dry with the kind of enveloping warmth that comes from an oven. The kilns had been fired before our arrival and were kept stoked day and night,
not for our comfort but for the firing of a load of pottery. After the ghastly cold of the road it felt wonderful just to be warm.

The stragglers from our column continued to drift in, small groups of prisoners and guards who finally abandoned their barns and milk-houses and stumbled, half-frozen, frost-bitten, and tired, into the town and the warmth of the pottery factory. But I slept. Without even spreading my blanket to make a bed, I slept on the bare boards of the factory floor.

When, at long last, my body had renewed its strength with sleep, hunger woke me. I had not been conscious of hunger during the march, nor of thirst either. I had eaten a bit of snow now and then, but that was to clear my head, not to satisfy a sense of need. Now, my whole being cried out for food and water. I was as dry as ever a desert could make me. The oven-like air had left me feeling parched as if I had indeed been in an oven.

I wandered about among the men, some sleeping, some eating, and others just staring into space, until I found a dripping water spigot. I turned it on and gulped the water greedily from my hand, letting the excess fall through my fingers into a puddle on the potter's table. I thought about the possibility that I might over-do it, but I drank until I could drink no more. Then I turned the spigot off again and went back to my pack to look for food.

Red Cross food parcels sometimes contained a ready-mixed cocoa that needed only hot water to make it into a very good-tasting and very nourishing drink. I dug into my pack and found a can that I didn't know was there. When we had left Sagan, we had been issued a food parcel each and I had hardly glanced at the items as I stowed them away. But here was cocoa just when I needed something quick and nourishing. I poured water in a tin can and mixed in the powder until the whole thing was only slightly thinner than a pudding and then drank it straight off. It was too sweet and the cloying taste of it had to be washed away with more water, but it gave me the quick energy that I needed just then.

As my energies revived, so did my curiosity. I began to take stock of my surroundings, evaluating everything in terms of its potential for an escape attempt. It was a habit bred of long months in captivity and by now had become as much a part of me as my own skin.

Not that I would necessarily make an attempt to escape, but I would always weigh its possibilities.

The factory seemed to be partially shut down while the kilns dried the latest products from the potter's wheels. The only non-prisoner people that I saw around were our guards, except for a lone fireman who made the rounds of the kilns, poking and spreading the coals of fire so that the burn would be even throughout.

He seemed an odd sort. Although he was young, probably not yet thirty, and able-bodied, he did not seem to be a part of any of the German military services. He did not even wear a uniform like the railway workers and other public employees did. Very peculiar indeed.

As I wondered about this and watched him going from kiln to kiln the answer slowly worked its way upward into my consciousness; he was a prisoner too! Not in the same sense that we were, but a prisoner nonetheless. At that time the Germans were using thousands of foreign workers in their industry: Poles, Frenchmen, Italians, Romanians; any of the conquered or allied areas was likely to contribute its share of manpower to the German state. And they were not much better off than slaves. They could go about unescorted by guards, but in all other things they were not any better off than we were. And, in many respects, may have been in worse condition.

So he was a prisoner of the Germans too! He might, therefore, be able to contribute some information on the potential for escapes. Like places to hide and ways to get out of the town without being seen. I made up my mind to try to engage him in conversation.

My opening effort involved putting myself in a position where I could logically speak to him without it looking like what it was: an attempt to get information. So I took a tin can of water to the kiln where he was busily raking the coals and spreading new fuel in the firebox. I stood near him until he had finished his work and straightened up, then I spoke in slow, clearly enunciated English.

"May I heat my water on the fire before you close the firebox?" I motioned toward the glowing grate with my can of water to indicate my meaning in case he didn't follow my question. I didn't really care if the water was heated or not, but I wanted him to talk so that I could get some idea of his understanding of my English. He looked at me with empty eyes, not having understood a word I said, knowing only that I had spoken to him and had waved a tin can about.

So I decided to try Spanish. I had arrived at the conclusion some time earlier that Spanish was enough to get one by anywhere in the southern part of Europe. Rightly or wrongly, I believed it was enough like French and Italian to do in a pinch, and this man had the look of an Italian to me. So I carefully framed my question in Spanish.

"*No lo capito*," was his immediate answer. His eyes were alive now but they were troubled, with the look of one who knows that something is required of him but is uncertain as to what it is. I repeated the question slowly.

"*No lo capito.*" His words meant nothing to me. I tried relating them to some expression in Spanish, but there just wasn't any comparable term that I could arrive at. I reworded my question and tried again.

"*No lo capito.*" He was beginning to worry about the goons who wandered about inside the building. I saw him glancing at them nervously as he repeated his plaintive answer.

I kept after it until I had exhausted my stock of ways to ask a single question and he was getting more nervous all the time. But his answer never varied: "*No lo capito.*"

Finally, thinking that perhaps we could put together a few sentences by mixing languages, I asked him: "*Parlez vous Francais*?" His answer was a stream of French that I had to have someone else translate for me. We had quite a long chat then, using A Louie as an interpreter. And we both laughed over the fact that I had thought he was Italian and he had thought I was speaking Italian!

"*No lo capito.*" Italian for "I don't understand."

Another man I met by chance in that pottery factory was a Brazilian. I never got it quite straight as to whether he had served in the Air Force of his own country or of some other, but it was unimportant at any rate. He had been taken prisoner six months before and had been tossed into the South Compound at Sagan with men who spoke little or no Portuguese. And his command of English was rudimentary at best.

But he did speak Spanish. He had grown up somewhere along the Argentine or Uruguay border where the two languages are used interchangeably. Hearing me trying to talk Spanish to a Frenchman, he was immediately attracted. He sidled over to listen, as we went through our translated conversation, and lingered on after the Frenchman had gone about his fire-tending.

He opened the conversation rather guardedly, probing to find out how much Spanish I would understand. But when he found that I could follow his words even when they came in a torrent, they did indeed come in a torrent. He followed me about all that day, talking incessantly. I had only to acknowledge now and again that I was following the line of his thought. There was no need for me to talk much; he did enough for both of us. The poor man had been living in a world of meaningless sound for those six months and at last he had found someone with whom he could communicate.

He stayed close by me when we left the pottery plant and seemed to take a special pleasure in being near me. After that first day it was no longer necessary to talk all the time. He would go for hours without speaking, but he never was far from me. And he would come back every day or so for a few words of conversation even after we got to Moosburg.

* * *

The weather and the Germans seemed to have

relented at the same time; the sun came out, the snow melted, and the Germans found transportation for us. In terms of creature comforts it wasn't much but, under the circumstances, we didn't refuse it. In a mood bordering on joyousness we walked through the slush of the spring thaw from our last stopping place to the rail line. We were to travel from there by train. We had no idea where we were going, but at least it would not be on foot.

"Forty and eight" is a term that has become part of the language since World War I when hundreds of thousands of Americans were moved about France in the all-purpose freight cars. I had grown up knowing the term as "*quarante hommes, huit chevaux* " because a family friend always referred to it that way. To me it meant a boxcar, but I envisioned it as something like ours; solid-sided, capacious, warm with the doors closed, cool and breezy with them open. I was not at all prepared for what we found when we got to the rail siding.

The cars sat on a double siding, lined up two-by-two in neat order as if some overly meticulous child had left his toys there. They were tiny things that didn't look capable of holding forty men standing erect, not even if they breathed in unison. And as for eight horses, I remembered the broad-backed draft horses of the farm and knew that nobody could put eight of them in one of those little boxcars. Hannah, a mule on my father's farm, would have occupied at least a quarter of one and she would have kicked the side out of it just to keep from feeling cramped.

They were made with solid ends, but the sides were slatted like cattle cars, leaving plenty of room for the vagrant breezes to wander through. The floors were covered with straw that looked like it had made several trips across the country hauling the latter half of the forty and eight combination. But it would be better than walking.

Or would it? The thought crossed my mind that trains were considered fair game and a great target of opportunity by fighter pilots. How could a pilot know that the cars he fired at contained prisoners? To him they would just be more of Jerry's war materiel. Maybe walking was better, after all. At least if the thaw continued.

The decision was not mine, of course. While I stood pondering the relative advantages of the two means of locomotion the order was given to board the boxcars. We were peeled out in groups of fifty and hustled into the cars. If I had thought forty men would have to breathe in unison, then fifty would have to double deck. But somehow they pushed and shoved us until all fifty were inside, then two guards forced their way in and the doors were closed and padlocked.

Then the situation got worse. The guards pushed and threatened until they had cleared a space as wide as the door and running across the car from door to door. This they roped off as their own space and left the other two-thirds of the car to the prisoners. We took small comfort in the fact that the lurching of the train was not likely to throw us off balance; no one could possibly fall in that pack!

But my purpose in telling this is not to gain sympathy. A description of the conditions of our travel seems necessary as a prelude to the incidents that followed on that ride. In the press of boarding I was squeezed into a corner of the car where I could see nothing to the front nor to my right, but had, just at eye level, a wide crack between two slats of the side of the car so that I could watch the countryside recede as the train puffed and wheezed its way southward. And it was through that crack that I saw the bombing of Chemnitz and through it I was witness to industry driven underground.

Up to this time I had been the bomber, not the bombed. There had been a few nights in England when the wail of sirens had sent us running to the air raid shelters, and there had been that interminable night when the *bahnhof* had sifted down around my ears, but mostly I thought of air raids in terms that were impersonal and professional.

But Chemnitz changed all that. We had wheezed into the railyard just at dusk and, for some reason, were kept standing on a siding for hours. Other trains came and went, but still we sat. Ours was obviously not priority cargo. Someone, out of kindness or sadism, I don't know which, had a barrel of water wheeled along the tracks so that we could dip out enough to slake our thirst. That it was water made it look like an act of kindness, but the slime that floated in it made it more an act of sadism.

Dusk turned to night and we could hear the sounds of the city around us and, here and there, we could see a glimmer of light where a black-out curtain had been left open. Switch engines chuffed and hissed back and forth with only the glow from their fires to light their way. Signalmen's lanterns gleamed momentarily and then were gone.

Far off in the distance I heard a faint wail that was taken up and repeated from a nearer point. It grew and grew until the insistent shriek of the sirens seemed to be beating against my eardrums from every side. There was a jostling of the train as if we were about to pull out, then utter motionlessness as the engine glided away alone. We had been uncoupled and left in the yard! Switch engines gleamed their fires on the rails as they gained speed, heading out of the yard to the comparative safety of open country.

And we were alone. All the little pools of light under uncurtained windows had suddenly gone out. No more signal lanterns flickered and the engine fires no longer laid a warm glow along the cinders. There was only the panic shrieking of the sirens and, far off, the throb of aircraft engines.

The first aircraft laid his flares, seemingly, just above our heads. I could not see the flares themselves, but I could see the suddenly light rail yard, its buildings and boxcars bathed in the cold, white light of burning magnesium. Its intensity and lack of shadows made it seem somehow accusatory and I wanted to hide, to dig a hole and withdraw into it. But how could one escape? Even our guards had to sit and take it. We were locked in and powerless to move.

A second plane droned over us, adding his flares to the first while the throbbing of prop tips against the air grew more urgent. There was no mistaking whose planes they were; only the British sounded like that, and only the British made raids in such an apparently haphazard pattern. The planes were all about us, coming in now from all directions and seeming to converge directly over our heads. The sound of the falling bombs played an obligato to the still shrieking sirens.

"Whu-umph! Whu-umph! Whu-umph!" They grunted as they turned over and over in mid-air and their turnings seemed an echo to the ululations of the sirens. I was absolutely convinced that we were at target center, destined to have our lives snuffed out in the next moment.

The first explosion happened to be directly in my line of vision. I was staring out into the dead-bright switchyard when a building half across the town exploded and sent debris swirling into the light of the chandelier flares. And then a second and a third explosion. The swarm overhead had thickened until it sounded a constant drum roll and the cloud of dust and debris over the town quickly blotted out all details.

The concussion of the first explosion hit us hard on the heels of its sound. The cars bounced and swayed along the tracks, impelled by the force of the bombs as if they were animated. I held my breath and waited for the crashing and grinding that would signal the breakup of the train. The second bomb's concussion hit before the first had died and we were pushed still further down the track toward the open country where our engine had taken refuge.

The bombs continued to fall in a torrent while we pitched and swayed through the rail yard. From my corner I could see other strings of cars careening along other tracks, pushed by the same concussive force that moved us. Once, almost beside me, two strings came to the junction of their switches and piled into one another, spilling railcars across half a dozen intervening tracks. But, miraculously, we moved on, untouched by the wreckage that surrounded us.

After an eternity, their fury spent and their bomb racks empty, the planes droned away and left the smoking city in the darkness. Our string of cars sat forlornly beside a line of dark trees on the very edge of the yard. We could be pushed no further, for there the track ended.

With dawn came the work brigades to clear the debris and get the tracks back into use again. They swarmed across the yard, tossing the wreckage into piles beside the tracks, marking the blocked tracks with little colored flags, and generally charting a way through the litter so that the trains could move again. And by noon our engine had found us again and began the slow process of backing and filling to work us out of the crippled city.

* * *

As we continued southward and westward the country seemed to become more mountainous. The engine labored almost constantly and our speed sometimes dropped to less than a good walk. The roadbed seemed to be following the course of a river most of the time and we occasionally ducked into a tunnel for a few seconds of pitch blackness.

Those seconds in tunnels were torture. The smoke from the engine was fanned back along the train and came billowing into our cars through the slatted sides, causing us to choke and cough until the train cleared the darkness and had time to exchange its load of coal smoke for fresher air.

It was during one of those fits of coughing that I saw the machine shop in the mountain. We had climbed high in the mountains near what had once been the Czech border and entered the tunnel at a crawl. The engine was laboring mightily to keep us moving and was laying down a solid cylinder of oily, black smoke that hung like a living thing beside the train. As we crept into the tunnel the coil of smoke invaded the cars, bringing tears to the eyes and a searing, wracking cough from the lungs.

Slowly, slowly the train moved forward. I could not see its progress in the darkness, but I could feel the motion as it creaked over the rails and I could hear the clack-clack of the trucks as they passed over the rail joints. My lungs felt as if they were ready to rupture for need of air and I felt dizzy.

Through the stinging tears I caught a glimpse of light and turned my head to see what it was. I really expected, indeed hoped, that it was the end of the tunnel and that I could soon be breathing clean air again. The light streamed in from my left and suddenly the air cleared.

It didn't last long, a few seconds at most while we clattered past, but it was enough to give me a single, startled look at what had happened to the German industry that we had been trying so hard to bomb out of existence. There, in row after row that stretched far back into the mountain, were the lathes and shapers and dies and molds that supplied the parts to keep the tanks of the *Panzer* divisions going. There, hidden in the mountain with only a railroad to mark its entrance, was a complete and functioning war plant. In an instant it was gone and we were back into the blackness of the tunnel with its smoke and grime.

Several days later the location of the factory was the subject of an effort by several of us who had seen it, to pinpoint it for possible relay to Allied Intelligence. I suppose the information must have gotten to the right people for I was told months later in France that a bomb was skipped into the entrance to seal the tunnel. I don't know if our efforts had anything to do with its destruction, but I have always felt that they did.

VI

Nuremberg

It was unexpectedly warm for a late-winter day. Yesterday's wind was stilled and the snows of Silesia were only a memory from two months past. Tiny spears of grass showed emerald through the tangled mass of last year's tattered growth. And in the cleared space between the fences a pigeon dusted himself.

Under the spell of the Bavarian sun and the soft air my mind floated free somewhere outside my real existence. I had learned early that the human spirit is not bound by its physical surroundings, but sets its own limits. And so I sat in the lee of the barracks enjoying the warmth and watching the slow, almost imperceptible reawakening of the world from a winter of hibernation. In spite of my weakened condition and my appalling filthiness I was enjoying the moment. In my mind ran a thread of music from somewhere, something somber, yet reassuring, echoing the agony of the past winter and, at the same time, the hope of the almost nightly air raids.

Yes, hope. One does not ordinarily think of being bombed as a hopeful situation. Yet we were cheered by the apparent ease with which the British were able to hit the town. It meant that the armies were closing in and somewhere over the horizon to the west there was freedom and an end to the war. So we watched the nightly display overhead and were reassured by the knowledge - or was it only hope? - that Intelligence had briefed the crews on our location.

Later we would be subjected to a merciless, three-times-a-day pounding by the combined fleets of the Allies, an assault that was to last for days and to bring the destruction to the very perimeter fence. But for now my mind was centered on the emergence of spring and food.

Each tiny spear of grass, each tightly furled leaf of dandelion represented food. Our diet for some time had been woefully deficient in the area of fresh vegetables and I searched my mind to dredge up all that I could remember about edible plants. Dandelions, I knew, were good food, even being considered a delicacy in some circles. But the quantity available did not look to be anywhere near adequate. They would have to be supplemented with other things and common meadow grass seemed a likely prospect.

My hungry planning was broken by the sounds of voices inside the barracks. The casement above my head was opened and carefully latched to the wall as a fragment of conversation drifted out. It seemed that the *feldwebel* had promised that we could shower today. The thought of it made me limp. To be clean again! To smell of soap and steaming water! Even cold water, so long as it would clean.

A shower is a simple thing that most of us take for granted. Cleanliness is the inalienable right of every man. Or at least that is the way we think now. But it is not so. Our last opportunity to bathe had been in Silesia two months before. Since that last bath we had tramped along miles of back-country roads, sleeping in barns and grateful for the warmth of the animals. We had ridden across the Sudeten and into Bavaria aboard the conventional forty-and-eight boxcars, always attended by overcrowding of human bodies and the stress of being captives. And we had vegetated in this awful camp whose nearest approach to the amenities of life was a honey bucket in the barracks entry.

We smelled.

No, we stank. Our unwashed bodies, our unwashed clothes, the clammy sweat that came unbidden in the night, these things combined to give us the aroma of camel drovers.

And many of us were no longer well. Our reduced diet had left us prey to every passing germ and, while we could not say that we were worse off than our guards, we found it difficult to appreciate the situation. We stank, and a bath was a luxury beyond imagining.

My mind luxuriated in the thought. To be clean, to rid oneself of the scaling skin that tokened too much exposure to cold and too little to water. To draw into the lungs the warm and steamy air of a bath, the sweet smell of soap. These thoughts conjured images to satisfy the body as well as the mind. I sat for a very long time in the sunshine enjoying the anticipation if not the fact.

I took off my shoes and carefully examined the stubborn infection that remained a painful evidence of frostbite acquired somewhere in the depths of a Silesian pine forest. Escape had been a hopeless thing at the time, but even the hopeless things must be tried. The price I paid was this lingering infection. I never knew if my captors considered my frostbite to be punishment enough or if they simply could not afford the time to administer any other. I hoped that a good cleaning would work the cure that so far had eluded me.

As my mind busied itself with anticipation it suppressed the remembered rumors and half-spoken hints that genocide was not unknown to my captors. The thoughts were suppressed and yet they resurfaced to be suppressed again, fragmentary thoughts of fragmentary remembrances. The voice of a trained goon who said of the Sagan shower room that its shower heads were "real." The hint that the Europeans in the compound across the fence from those "real" shower heads were on their last stop before execution. The dispassionate discussions about the cost of keeping us as opposed to liquidation. And finally, the order that liquidation was to be the course taken, and the countermanding of that order when its full consequences to the German nation became apparent. These things we had heard in bits and pieces, without confirmation. And they came to my mind in the same fashion. I would not admit these disjointed forebodings to the stream of my thoughts, but they remained just below the level of consciousness like floating snags in a peaceful river.

A shower was not to be on that day. Our informant apparently had misunderstood, for noonday dragged on into afternoon without a hint of activity in the *vorlager*. We went about our business, such as it was, first with an unaccustomed briskness and then, as it became increasingly apparent that there would not be time for the trip out to the shower and back before night, we moved with a mixture of disappointment and relief. We were disappointed that our shower was not to be and relieved that we did not have to face that shower head, uncertain as to its "realness."

I speak of the trip "out" to the shower as if it were a natural thing and, to us at the time, it was. We understood and accepted as normal the fact that there were no bathing facilities anywhere within the vast compound including even the *vorlager*, that center of our world through which all orders must come. Our information and understanding was that we would be taken in groups of manageable size to the cantonment area where our guards lived, and there we would bathe. We had no idea where this area might be, but we were sure that it would be well-guarded. There were whispered discussions of attempts to escape if the opportunity came, but they were half-hearted and more wishful thinking than actual plans.

At last when evening headcount came our last hopes died, for the guards lined up in the *vorlager* exactly as they did twice a day, every day of our lives. They obviously were intent only on counting us to be sure that no one had managed to slip away when they were not looking. This twice a day headcount remains a monument to Prussian military rigidity. It was a formality which was not abandoned, even when we were locked into boxcars in a moving train.

And so we were counted. We did not even engage in our usual practice of forcing a recount by moving about in ranks. Something in our spirit died when the *vorlager* gate swung open to admit the *appell* guard. We were destined to keep our filth and grime to the end of our captivity. Our disappointment was lightened only by the certain knowledge that the war was drawing to its final conclusion and that, if we could but survive, we would eventually be free.

But *Hauptman* Eiler was a man with a sense of the dramatic. When the final count had been tallied and the *feldwebel* had confirmed that none had escaped, when the last salute had been exchanged with the Senior Officer, he turned, not to the *appell* guard which had formed up ready to leave, but toward the assembled prisoners and waited for silence. It came with a sudden rush, like a quiet wind, over the ranks. This was a most unprecedented thing. The *hauptman* obviously wanted to speak to us and we responded with a silence that was compounded of expectation and dread.

He only spoke five words in his halting English. But those five words were enough to set off a roar of approval that startled the pigeons from the roofs of the *vorlager* and sent them swirling about like chaff in the wind.

"Tomorrow you bathe. I promise," he said. And when the din of the cheers had died away he had gone through the *vorlager* gate and the *appell* guard was hurrying to catch up.

That night we lay awake long past lock-up time. The darkness was filled with a murmuring that was not so much conversation as anticipation.

With sunrise came the morning headcount. We assembled eagerly, forming ranks without our usual shuffling and moving about. For today we wanted to have nothing interfere with our chance to be clean again. Uncooperative behavior could be the excuse for not being allowed a bath. The count moved so quickly, the total tallied so properly, that the *hauptman* considered a recount on the theory that there must be something wrong. Never before had he been able to get a correct count on the first try. We could see the progress of the discussion with the *feldwebel*, we could interpret the meaning of the gestures, even though we could not hear their words. We waited, half resigned to being recounted even though we were impatient to be on the way to the shower.

Finally, having satisfied himself that there were indeed the proper number of prisoners present and accounted for, the *hauptman* gave the word to proceed. The *feldwebel* moved to the center of the line and gave us our instructions. We were to be marched to the showers in groups of thirty, beginning with the lowest numbered barracks and proceeding upward. No group of thirty was to be permitted to leave the compound with less than six guards. No one would be permitted to leave the undressing area until all were ready to leave. An on and on he droned, giving us the minute details, the petty rules to govern that most personal operation, the bath.

My group was the second one to leave the compound so I did not have long to spend in anticipation. When the call came we dashed into the assembly area by the gate and formed into three ranks instantly, as if we were a crack drill squad. Our six guards took their places on either side of us and we swept through the gate like a small town parade.

We turned right and left on command, having no idea where the showers were located. And we kept a clear eye to the front, for we expected to meet the first group on their way back to camp. The road was unpaved and dusty, and where it passed through a section of wood the morning air was chill. I have no idea how far it was for my mind was busy with anticipation and I lost all track of time. I carefully examined each building that we approached for any evidence of its function. Each one I was sure contained the showers and each one in turn proved to serve some other purpose: a storehouse, a group of barracks, even a farm barn incongruously tucked into this maze of prison compounds and administrative areas.

We came at last to a group of wooden barracks for all the world like those we had left. This could be another compound of the prison. But it could not be the right place. The *feldwebel* had said the cantonment area. And yet the guards ordered us to a halt while one of them went into one of the buildings. Suddenly, all of the fears of yesterday sprang into my mind and wrenched me into an alertness that was animal-like. This was a *vorlager*! The fence behind those buildings was double and the tops tilted in to hinder climbing. I could not see it, but my imagination knew just where the concertina wire would be, and the trip-wire on the inside of the whole thing. The Cooler was just to the left of the administrative hut, the kennels behind it. The goon towers jutted above the whole thing like monstrous hobgoblins.

We waited. There was nothing else we could do. But my eyes roved the area looking for some possibility of escape. And as I looked I knew that it would be a futile effort. For the goon towers were double-manned and dogs patrolled the area outside the fence. Just for a fleeting moment I remembered the crumpled form dangling from the fence in Sagan, but I forced the memory away. It would not do to remember such things.

Then we were ordered to move. As we rounded the first building we saw what had escaped us before. In the center of the *vorlager* was a stone building, low-roofed and almost windowless. It could be the gun vault, or it could be the shower room, or it could be anything. Its exterior told me nothing. Or almost nothing. But the cold fear remained.

And so we came into the building to find the *feldwebel* and more guards waiting inside the room. It was a bare room, with only a long bench and pegs around the walls for hanging clothes. I was relieved to recognize the atmosphere. It smelled of steam and strong soap, and, at the same time, of unwashed bodies and clothing. I could have cried in my relief except for the nagging thought that we had not seen the first group as we expected. Where were they? Why had we not seen them along the road? If they were still here, where was the evidence of them? My mouth was dry from fear and my mind seemed racing out of control.

When every man was stripped and ready for the shower, trembling with a mixture of anticipation and fear, the *feldwebel* threw open the door and we were engulfed in steam. My fear-dried throat relaxed as the warm vapor swirled through the room and I saw, through the mists, the last of group one being herded out by the guards.

* * *

Stalag XIII-D was not a country club. Some said that it had been converted from its original use as a Nazi party parade ground to serve as a detention area for those Italian officers and men whom the Germans did not feel they could trust. They were allies, but they could not be trusted. So the camp was built to keep them away from the general population and, incidentally, keep them under surveillance.

Or so the story goes. I really don't know why nor how the camp was originally built. I only know that it was, in and of itself, a form of torture. The ramshackled buildings were crammed full of triple deck bunks built without space between them so that they served more as human storage bins than as beds. The washroom and shower buildings had long ago been dismantled by the occupants so that their frames and siding could be used for fuel. Some of the latrines had suffered a similar fate.

There were no air-raid shelters in the compound. I suppose there were shelters in the area where the goons lived, but there were none for us. And we really thought nothing of that fact, for we had not been subject to bombings up to that time. If you discount the false air-raid in the Silesian forest, that is. And that raid on the Frankfurt *bahnhof*. And Chemnitz. But that had been a long time ago.

The first planes came at night. First the air-raid sirens wailed, then the lights went out. Ten minutes later and without any plausible reason for it, they went on and were flicked off again almost immediately. We could hear the drone of aircraft engines in the distance, but had no way of knowing if it was ours or theirs. The goons along the perimeter fence kept shouting to us to close the shutters and stay inside.

Suddenly the drone of engines became louder and one single bomber streaked overhead, leaving a string of chandelier flares in his wake. Hard on his heels came a second plane and a second string of flares. Then the clusters of colored smoke flares that marked ground zero for the bombers to follow.

And they were not far behind. From the sounds of their engines we took them to be Lancasters while the pathfinders, the flare ships, had been Mosquitos. But we could not see them for it was pitch black outside and we dared not lean out the windows for fear that the guards would shoot. They came droning in, adding the throom-throom-throom sounds of their props to the constant din of the anti-aircraft guns. They were high - much higher than the lighter and faster flare ships had been, and perhaps that is what threw the gunners off in their aim, for their shots twinkled in the night sky and pelted the roof with spent flak, but they seemed to miss the raiding planes entirely.

It was a small raid as such things go - a couple of squadrons at the most, certainly not more than three. But it was a harbinger of things to come. And its significance was not lost on those of us who watched from the ground. Next day we set up a clamor for air-raid shelters. Our senior officers took the request to the German authorities and got nothing. They argued, cajoled, and quoted the Geneva Convention, but it did no good. The Germans had neither the manpower nor the equipment to spare. The best we got was permission to dig our own if we could manage it without tools!

We dug our own. With tin cans and fingernails and sharpened boards stolen from the side of the barracks we dug our own. The goons came by and watched, making sure that we didn't dig any tunnels instead of air-raid trenches, but they didn't interfere. And within a week we could feel fairly secure, having clawed out enough trenches and foxholes to take care of everyone.

And every man devised some method to protect himself from the spent shrapnel that rains down during such a raid. Some kept folded blankets to be used as a head cover in the trenches, others carried wooden stools for the same purpose. A few chose to stay inside the barracks rather than risk the spent flak.

During that week when we were digging and clawing at the earth we had no more raids. There were a few alerts when Allied fighters showed up overhead and once we hustled into the trenches when a lone P-38 made a reconnaissance flight over the town, obviously making pictures. But no bombs were dropped.

We were beginning to feel a little foolish for our panic, wondering what had gone wrong to cause the Allied advance to slow down, when the tempo changed and we had no longer to doubt the wisdom of our trenches. Beginning with another night raid we were pounded mercilessly, three-times-a-day, for over a week.

I say we were pounded mercilessly. We, as such, were not bombed directly. It was obvious, even as we shivered in our shelters, that the planners back in London knew that we were there and had briefed the crews accordingly. Always the path to the target was routed so that no stray bomb could become dislodged and accidentally fall into our camp. And we had the feeling that the nearest line of chandelier flares marked the edge of the permissible drop zone. Anyone who dropped a bomb on the wrong side of that line was likely to have a lot of explaining to do.

Somehow we felt safer during the daylight raids. Perhaps it was the fact that the attackers were American. Or that we could see them and, by extension, assumed that they could see us. Whatever the psychology of the thing, we felt safer in the light and, in a sense, we probably were. The American raids confined themselves to standard ordinance - frags, five hundred pounders, and thousand pounders. The concussion from their explosions was enormous, enough so that it was wise to stay below ground level to protect your eardrums. But they were predictable things - the strings of bombs were dropped simultaneously, the explosions came in a chain, and when they were done they were done.

But the British raids were something else again. They used bombs of enormous size, and fuses that, from the standpoint of the man on the receiving end at least, were wholly unpredictable. The whole thing might explode before it really hit ground or it might burrow deep into the bowels of the earth before going off with a roar that would shake half the town. After one of their raids we were never certain when it would be safe to come out of the trenches and go back to bed. Another bomb might go off at anytime.

I don't mean to seem critical of their methods. I have a great respect for the men who flew those missions. And their efforts contributed mightily to the downfall of the Third Reich. But when you are sitting in a hole in the ground wondering if the last bomb has exploded, sometimes it is hard to be objective.

* * *

My memory for specific dates is rather blurred. I could not with any certainty tell you if it was the night of any specific date on which I watched a Lancaster spiral down out of control, almost certainly carrying the crew to their deaths. But my memory of the event, the visual and auditory memory, is as clear today as if I had just witnessed it.

The air-raid sirens had brought us out of our beds early that night. Many of us, in fact, had not yet gone to bed but were poking about in the half-darkness of the barracks waiting for the inevitable sirens, but hoping that tonight they would stay quiet. We had our blankets and our stools at the ready, but we hoped not to need them. Our nerves were wound tight from the constant strain of being under bombardment and we found it difficult to sleep soundly, even when all was calm and silent outside. We badly needed a night's sleep. But that was not to be. The first siren began its coyote call ahead of schedule, sounding lonely and distant. The song was taken up by those nearer and nearer until the wail of the combined sirens seemed to envelop us and to hold us in a web of intolerable sound. Slowly, slowly the wailing moved over and past us into the town and beyond. As it died out in the distance we could hear the first planes faintly.

The German gunners that night had help. Previously, the *Luftwaffe* had chosen to stay on the ground rather than risk the losses that would have been inevitable. Or perhaps the bombing was taking its toll of their oil supplies. Whatever the reason, they had not risen to meet the night raiders on other nights, but that night they did. At least a dozen, maybe more, of the night-fighters wheeled and turned in the night sky, sending ribbons of tracer fire arching toward the sounds of the bombers. And the bombers in their turn spewed fountains of flickering fire from every gun-mount. It could have been described as beautiful if it had not been so deadly.

Almost directly over our heads a fighter suddenly erupted in flame, its throbbing pulse beat changing to a scream as it went out of control. Like a Fourth of July rocket in reverse it arched downward, trailing fire and debris as it disintegrated. From along the line of trenches came the muttered malediction of: "Auger in, you bastard!"

Even as we watched him auguring in we realized that his nemesis had fared no better than he did, for the bomber above us was obviously in trouble. The engines were surging wildly and the erratic path he seemed to be following indicated repeated loss of control. We could not see him in the blackness, but we could follow his movements more or less by sound, for the ground guns were silent while the night-fighters were at work.

Then an engine caught fire. We never knew if it was a result of the attack of the first fighter or if another had slipped in without our notice. But the tail of flames gave us a visual reference to match the sounds of the heaving and pitching plane. The men who had cheered a moment before when the German plane spun in were silent now, holding their breath, and willing the plane to right itself. Beside me in the trench George muttered "No! No!" under his breath and drove his fist into the hard dirt of the wall as if to force his will on the thing that was happening above us.

The flames spread and we saw the disintegration begin as a part of the wing peeled off, momentarily lighted by the conflagration before it swirled away into the darkness. The plane, not really under control since the initial attack, now was a brilliant leaf swirling downward on an autumn wind. We watched, spellbound and helpless, as it spiraled into the ground and exploded among the buildings of Nuremberg. In spite of everything, including death, he had put his bomb load on the target.

* * *

There were other nights and other days when terror was the most common state of mind among us, nights and days of constant bombing and near misses. Bit by bit the town visible across the fence changed from distinct buildings and streets and bridges and street lamps to a smoking rubbish heap. Great gaping holes showed in the forest on the other side where stray bombs had dropped accidentally, spraying pine trees about like jackstraws. One dropped so close that it demolished a goon tower and ripped a barracks off its foundation, but, aside from minor wounds from falling shrapnel, no one was hurt.

When there was nothing left to bomb, when smoke from the unchecked fires obscured the wreckage that had been a town, the bomb raids finally stopped. And the people crept out of their hiding places and began to move about on the other side of our fences. The clean-up operation was under way.

VII

Evacuation of Nuremburg

The decision to evacuate *Stalag* XIII-D was announced at morning *appell*. It was a decision that most of us had been expecting but had hoped would not come. If only we could be left in place a few days, a few weeks longer the Allied armies surging in from the west would over-run the area and we would again be free. If only. But we did not expect that to happen. Not just yet nor just in this place. We had long ago faced the fact that the Germans would make one more effort to keep us, would make one more effort to move us deeper into the shrinking Third *Reich*. That we would move on foot did not surprise us, either. There was no longer any other way available.

Preparing for the move took no time at all. How long does it take to pack all of one's possessions? Not long when they consist of six cans of food, half a loaf of black bread, a spare shirt, and a carefully preserved notebook. We each, at any given moment, stood in most of our wardrobe so packing our clothing was nothing. And the goons never allowed us to accumulate any excess food so there was not much to pack there either. The upshot of it all was that every man was ready for the move within fifteen minutes of the announcement.

Though we did not move gladly it was not for love of XIII-D that we dallied. For the two months that we had been here this had qualified in every way as a pest-hole. There was the crowding — men warehoused in bins with no regard for the bare essentials of sanitation or health, the sick and the well intermingled so that, after a time, they were indistinguishable; all were to some degree sick. And there was the lack of food — the supply of Red Cross parcels was sporadic and unpredictable, and the goon rations were mostly inedible when we got them and sometimes we didn't get them at all.

And then there were the bugs. The very buildings seemed to be held together by vermin. Bed bugs filled every available crack and crevice, and the beds seemed to be stuffed with body lice instead of straw. In such a situation one does not sleep, but goes into a state of suspended animation, exhausted by the effort to fight off the bugs.

We were not sad to see the last of *Stalag* XIII-D. But from the very beginning we played a stalling game. It had been the *hauptman's* intention to get the column moving by ten o'clock, but it was well nigh noon before he got the first of the prisoners started down the road toward Neumarkt. We found a thousand reasons to delay, hoping that somehow we could still be overtaken by the Allied spearhead.

Slowly, grudgingly we formed ranks and began the trek. The goons knew that they were no longer in real control of the situation, that our roles might be reversed at any time so that they would be the prisoners and we the keepers. And they were not inclined to push their luck. We insisted on frequent rest breaks and they agreed. We demanded a slower pace and they agreed.

We insisted on extra time for lunch and they agreed to that too.

But lunch was late in coming even at that. We had not left the camp until noon and were clamoring for a lunch break almost immediately, so that the *hauptman* agreed that we would stop at the first village outside of Nuremburg. His intention was good, but the dive bombers made it impossible to live up to. The sirens began their wailing before the first column had cleared the outskirts of the town and were reaching a crescendo by the time we reached Postbaur, some two kilometers further on. As the column slowly collapsed into itself and into Postbaur, we heard the whine of the distant aircraft and the staccato drumming of the ack-ack guns.

They came hurtling in toward us like angry hornets, their undersides lumpy with their external racks and bombs. They were not high as fighters usually were; they were low enough that we could identify them and could count the bombs along their wings. And they were obviously beginning their bomb run. We were their target!

I don't remember a command being given, but there must have been one. Suddenly the entire mass of humanity was forming itself into the letters POW. The guards, too, joined in the effort to identify ourselves and to warn away the bombers. They crowded in with us to form the letters and some of them produced from somewhere, only they knew where, some strips of white cloth to use to form letters in an open field.

But the target, the real target, was the rail yard we had passed through a few minutes earlier. The P-47s passed over us and then dived toward the tracks below them. Time after time they sent their bombs plummeting into the maze of switches and standing trains, filling the air with the dust and debris and noise of explosions.

We were in no real danger now, so our guards began to round us up and to try to establish some sort of order. Men were sent to retrieve the strips of cloth and a guard line was posted around the open area where we were to take our lunch break. But most of us had lost interest in lunch. We sat along the sides of the road and in the fields, watching the progress of the bombing raid.

I for one, and I think a great many others as well, was fascinated by the concussion rings thrown out by the explosions. Visible concussion rings. I had seen that phenomenon a few times from the air, but now I was seeing it from ground level. I was seeing it and I was feeling it and I was hearing it. It began at the point of bomb impact as a white doughnut that spread outward at the speed of sound. You saw it coming toward you and you tensed your muscles in anticipation. There was the sledge hammer blow to the diaphragm by the onrush of air past you, followed by the deafening sound of the explosion itself. And you could see the ring as it rushed on into the distance until you lost it in the general haze. And your head still rang from the din of it and your heart hammered inside your chest as if to make up for that one moment when it had stood still under the punishing blow of concussion.

When the Thunderbolts had dropped their last bombs and had streaked away at treetop level, a pair of Lightnings, P-38s, swung lazily over the devastation of the rail yard. They were making damage assessment pictures, I'm sure, but it was as if they were casual sightseers. They were throttled back to a point just above stalling and they turned this way and that as they poked about above the debris. They looked for all the world like two old ladies at a rummage sale, gossiping and pointing out bargains to one another. Then, their curiosity satisfied, they too streaked away above the trees.

But in a minute or two we saw them hanging on their props as they clawed their way up to thinner air. Lunch was over and we must move on.

We must move on. To give the *hauptman* his due I must say that he made a valiant try at getting us on the road, but we pulled out all the stops in our delaying technique. Those who had genuine ailments grew worse and those of us who had no real complaints suddenly developed some. We had everything from swollen feet to severe intestinal cramps. So the *hauptman* gave in and we slept that night in the sweet hay of the barns of Postbaur.

* * *

She was old and worn. The skin of her face hung in little wrinkled pouches where once the flesh had been smooth and firm. Her faded blue eyes seemed to peer out at the world from the depths of their sunken sockets. Her once-blonde hair was now a yellowed grey and was piled haphazardly into a loose knot on the top of her head. Her dress could best be described as mid-thirties dowdy. And her desiccated form no longer filled it, so that it hung in pouches like the skin of her face.

She stood in the lamplight of the entryway, peering out at my wet and bedraggled state, and I could not tell if her intent was to order me away or not. Her manner gave me no hint. But she opened the door enough to let the light fall on my face and wet clothes.

I had come to her recessed doorway purely by accident. Our guards had seen fit to release us within the walls of the village of Berching. Of course, there was no real chance that any of us would escape because the village was completely surrounded by a medieval wall, which was now surmounted by the *Luftwaffe* guards. It was a kindness they extended us by implication; if we should choose to look for some friendly house along the way to the church where we were supposed to be billeted, then our guards would not have to feel embarrassed at saying no. And our potential host would not be open to censure either. They were not a bad lot, really, and their sympathy for our situation was only partly due to the distant sound of Patton's big guns.

So, as I said, I came to her doorway quite by accident. I was wet and exhausted from the long march of the night before, and I moved into the shelter of the entry while I got my bearings about me and relocated the spire of the church. I really had no thought of doing anything more than finding that church and getting dry and warm again. But I must have leaned against the door because it opened slightly, letting a trickle of warm air out against my neck. I wanted to push the door open and rush in to the source of that heat, but my common sense told me no. So I stood there a moment, unwilling to leave that tiny current of warmth, but knowing that I had to go on to the church before I could really get dry.

It could only have been a moment that I stood there before she opened the door. Perhaps she had seen me coming down the street and had come to the door to watch me pass. They often did that -- they came out to watch us go by as if, by watching, they could insure our speedy departure. Allied airmen were not popular figures in Bavaria just then, particularly since the bombing raids had begun to go after small town targets. Or perhaps she came out of curiosity like the mother and son who came to peek through the grate at me in Burg — came simply to look at the *Terrorflieger* in the way one goes to the zoo to see an elephant. Whatever her reason, she was there and she had opened the door so that the light and warmth seemed to envelop me. And she stood peering at me noncommittally.

"*Komme*," she said suddenly, and without waiting to see if I followed, she turned and went back up the hallway and through the only open door. I closed the front door carefully and followed. As I came into the room the whole of it seemed to be filled with one gigantic, porcelain stove. For those who have never seen such a stove this may sound like something out of a Marc Chagal painting, but it was real and it was warm and its tiles gleamed from floor to ceiling with dainty blue flowers and arabesques and curlicues. And as I entered she bent to open the grate and stoke the fire a bit to make it warmer.

My German was not really all that good and her English was nonexistent, but she ordered me to take off my clothes so that she could dry them. And I understood. All languages come easier when you are cold and wet, especially if it means a chance to get warm. There were others in the room, lying swaddled in their blankets on the chairs and on the floor. A pair of German army boots stood drying next to American shoes. The blankets all seemed to be prison-issue, however, so I assumed that one of the guards had slipped in to rest, hoping his superiors would not miss him. A trained goon, perhaps.

I set my pack down beside the door and took out my blanket. But the pack was leaving a wet spot on the floor so I moved it out into the hall where the floor was tile. Then I wrapped myself in the blanket and took off my clothes. She took each garment as I handed it to her and draped it about one of the twin stacks of the stove where it promptly sent out a cloud of steam And last she took my shoes and set them beside the *Wehrmacht* boots. The pervasive warmth of the place began to work on me and I fell asleep on the floor.

I spoke of the cold, wet march of the night before and perhaps that needs explaining. As evening fell we had come into a small farming village indistinguishable from those of the previous nights. We had been assigned our billets and our guards had taken their stations as they always did. We had gone about the business of arranging our meager gear and getting small fires started for our cooking. And we had met in groups of three and four to plan the usual trading forays.

I had just gathered up the soap and cigarettes, which were my contribution to the trade goods and was stashing them in the pockets of my coat, ready to turn them over to George, when I saw the *hauptman* scurry down the street and across a barnyard. I stopped to watch, as much out of wonder as anything else. I didn't want him to see me pass the trade goods, but the thing that made me stop was not fear. It was the fact that *Hauptman* Eiler never hurried. He always walked as if he were wound up like a clock spring that must proceed at its proper ticking. But there he was, scurrying, almost at a run, crossing the barnyard to the colonel's billet.

I waited. I had no alternative. With the *hauptman* in the barn I didn't dare go looking for George. All my pockets bulged suspiciously and I knew that George would be hard-pressed to hide what he already had collected.

Then they came out into the light, the colonel and the *hauptman*. They walked very quickly into the street and stood talking in low voices, glancing occasionally back up the road toward the last town we had passed through. I could not hear what they said, but their manner indicated a conferring rather than commanding.

Suddenly the *hauptman* seemed to reach a decision. He straightened to his full five feet six inches, spun on his heel and strode a few paces toward the nearest guard. The half-frightened man opened his mouth to say, "*jawohl, mein hauptman,*" but he never got it out. Eiler almost shrieked at him: "*Appell! Appell!*"

"*Appell! Appell!*" The cry was taken up by guards and prisoners alike until the bedlam of it had everyone out into the roadway milling about. Even the civilians came out onto their doorsteps to see what was going on. *Hausfrauen* and *kinder* hung from upper windows and tittered back and forth to each other. They were as much in ignorance as we were about the cause of it all.

And so it was that we were ordered to pick up our few belongings and prepare to move on. There was no attempt to hide the real fear in the *hauptman's* face as he told us, half in English and half in German, that we were in very real danger. That last town contained a rest camp for the *Wehrmacht* and its current occupants had just been badly mauled by Patton's army. And they were out for revenge. Some of them had been spotted moving through the countryside, armed and spoiling for trouble. Looking for Americans. The *hauptman* did not have enough guards to keep us in line properly and certainly could not hope to defend us from a mob of vengeful soldiers.

And so we fled. We literally ran until our lungs were screaming for air. And then we walked until we could get our breath back. And then we ran again. And the guards ran with us. If someone stumbled in the dark, the nearest man helped him to his feet. It might be prisoner or guard, it made no difference. Every man was running in fear.

Somewhere along the road the rain came. When we were all so completely exhausted that we thought we could not go any further, the rain came to make our lives even more difficult. And so we slogged on, fearful to stop at any of the villages, praying for dawn so that we could see if we were still being followed. The rain seeped in around our necks and plastered our pants to our shanks. Our un-dubbed shoes soon took on the feel of wet chamois. And still the rain came down.

In the grey light of morning we came to Berching, and I found her door and sleep.

I was always a light sleeper. Rain on the roof brings me instantly awake, at least long enough to know what the sound is. But her bustling in and out of the room with more wet stragglers did not bother me that day. I slept the sleep of exhaustion.

When I woke the room was crowded with people and smelled of damp wool and unwashed bodies. She moved silently around the room, returning dried shirts to their rightful owners, setting newly cleaned boots beside the proper sleeper, and stoking the fire to new life in that wonderful porcelain stove. As I dressed — she had laid my folded and dry clothing beside me while I slept — I watched her and wondered if she knew why we had come into her life like this. Did she know that we had fled in terror from the mob that was her army, an army that might even include her relatives, grandsons perhaps? Was she aware that we constituted a danger to her and hers? Did she not know the punishment meted out to those who helped an enemy?

If the *Wehrmacht* should find us there what would they do to her?

I wondered about those things, but there really was nothing I could do. And, besides, I was hungry. Then the realization came that it was well into the afternoon and I had not eaten since noon of the day before, and only a cold boiled potato then. I scrounged through my pack until I found that bit of bread that was to have been part of last night's supper. I ate it slowly, savoring each mouthful. It was the last of that beautiful white loaf I had bought from a farmwife for a few cigarettes. It had a robust flavor of good wheat flour and yeast, not like the sawdust and millet variety we often got.

But the bread raised a thirst. After a moment's consideration I took out my jar of instant coffee. I had no cup, only a tin can converted for use as a coffee cup, but that made it easier to heat water in it. I had intended to fill my can with water and set it on the ledge at the top of the stove to heat, but, as I stood up with the coffee in my hand, I saw the look in her eyes. It was a momentary thing, a purely involuntary reaction that she covered instantly, but it told me she could not refuse if I offered her some of my coffee.

You must understand that the war had cut Germany off from most of the commerce of the world. That food which could not be grown must be done without or must be simulated. And they were ingenious in their simulations. *Ersatz* honey made from coal tar supplemented the natural thing and was difficult to distinguish from it. But *ersatz* coffee was another thing. We were told that it was made from acorns and, from its taste, it was easy to believe. It tasted like pure tannic acid. But in the absence of the real thing the Germans drank it.

"*Wollen sie kaffee haben*?" I *asked* her, trying hard to sound casual. And as I said it I indicated the cups along a cup rail above the window. I wanted her to understand that I was offering a cup of coffee, not the whole jar. She smiled at me but did not answer, seeming to weigh the question, unable to resolve the conflict in her mind.

"*Ist wirklich, nicht ersatz,*" I encouraged her. She wavered a moment more in doubt and then gave in to her craving.

"*Danke,*" she said as she took two cups down from the rack and pushed the kettle to a warmer spot. Then she moved into the hallway and spoke to someone else. I could not follow the meaning of what she said, but I caught the name "*Karl*" and the word "*keller.*" I remembered those German boots drying before the stove that morning and wondered if Karl was their owner. Or was he perhaps her husband?

She came back into the room and busied herself with arranging two chairs so that we could sit at the table without disturbing any of the sleepers. And she brought spoons and a tiny pitcher of milk. There was no sugar. No one expected that sort of luxury. She had just set the pitcher of milk on the table and settled into her chair when a door behind the stove opened and Karl came up from the cellar. If I had expected her husband I was certainly wrong, for he was a good twenty years her junior although he was himself well into middle age. And if I had expected a trained goon I was even wider of the mark, for he wore the uniform of the *Wehrmacht,* not the *Luftwaffe.* For one startled instant I wanted to take to my heels and run as we had done the night before, and I suppose it must have shown in my face, for he smiled at me and spoke in English.

"We do not harm you. She is my mother. I have *schnapps* for your coffee." It was the sort of jumbled conversation that comes of a language learned from school books combined with a genuine desire to reassure. His face was kind and open; only the uniform looked menacing. And even that was worn with a casualness that betrayed the habits of his farm background. He set the bottle of schnapps on the table and started back toward the cellar door, saying something to his mother in German about finishing his work before he left.

He came back later, having finished some chore

in the barnyard, and joined us for a second cup of coffee. His English and my German made a conversation possible although it required a great deal of repetition and the occasional use of a word or two of French to shore up our meanings. But it was a conversation, and others joined in now and then to ask a question or to offer a translation one of us had missed. All in all, it took the edginess out of the closeness of men who, technically, were at war with one another.

He was a member of what we would describe as the Home Guard, those too old or too lame to serve in the active army but delegated to the task of maintaining internal order. Not a policeman in the strictest sense, yet a policeman of sorts. His age — he must have been approaching fifty — and his physical condition — it was several minutes before I realized that his left sleeve was empty — kept him from the active *Wehrmacht*, but it did not relieve him of a responsibility to serve the State. And there was also his mother's farm to be cared for.

Too soon he rose, saying that he must go to work and offering, if we wished, to walk with us to the church. It was not said unkindly, as a way to terminate the occupation of his mother's kitchen. Rather, it was a genuine offer to be helpful. Our guards would soon be searching everyone out anyway, because it was time to move on toward the south.

Together we walked the hundred yards or so to the church after saying our thanks to his mother. She stood in the doorway and watched us go and she was still standing there when we turned a corner that took us out of sight of her home.

Karl left us at the church door and strode across the square to the *polizeiwache* with his empty sleeve swinging at his side.

* * *

We moved slowly southward, becoming more demanding as our guards became more tolerant. We set up a scheme for estimating our distance from the front lines using timings taken from the flashes of explosions plotted against the time it took for the sound to reach us. And we began to slip out at night to trade our soap and cigarettes with the civilian population in exchange for food. If we were caught we risked losing what food we had acquired, but there was not likely to be any severe punishment. Not with Patton so close on our heels.

And we began to make impromptu escapes. I say impromptu because, up to that time, escape attempts had been coordinated through a committee which provided all of the necessary identity papers and clothing to make it possible to pass as European. But that was no longer necessary. The word was passed that unsanctioned escapes would be permitted and covered when possible, but that it would probably be wiser to wait for liberation by the advancing Third Army. Wisdom not withstanding, our numbers decreased each night and those of us remaining shuffled and milled about at *appell* in order to cover the escapes.

And we became aware that we were under surveillance by the Allied Forces. Each day we saw the reconnaissance planes as they flew over, at first very high but gradually getting lower and lower as the evidence of opposition diminished. A pair of P-51s made the flight each morning and each afternoon, obviously checking on the progress of the move for they flew a lazy S pattern down the length of the entire column. We made bad jokes about their coming to check the quality of our cooking, but their presence gave our spirits a lift that made those last days and weeks of waiting more tolerable.

It was beautiful country through which we were passing, rolling hills covered with thick woods, open grain fields waiting for spring planting and, here and there, the telltale poles and wires of hop fields. Along the roadside the grass was greening and early wildflowers were beginning to bud. In mid-afternoon the sun warmed us so that we took off our coats and opened our shirts to let the soft air in.

We seemed suspended in time. While the Germans tried to hurry us we stalled and tarried. And each day we seemed to move not at all in relation to the front lines. If we walked ten kilometers to the southeast, Patton advanced ten kilometers to the southeast; if we walked five kilometers south, Patton came the same distance to the south. There was that tantalizing rumble and clatter just over the horizon which never seemed to come any nearer.

It was with this sense of the world suspended that we had set out that morning from some nameless village to another nameless village. The road was a narrow country lane, hardly more than a track really, which wound from farm to farm on its way to nowhere. It shifted and turned from open field to wooded hillside and now and again picked up the course of a small stream which burbled and chuckled over its stony bed. We were to bathe in that stream later, but for now our only use of it was for drinking water. It was clear and pure and sparkling.

In bright afternoon sun we entered a wood. The trees were thick and straight on both sides of the road and, for a change, the road itself was straight. The forest was dark and foreboding, but the cleft made by the road was splashed with sunshine where it made a high embankment across a narrow little valley. The sides of the road fell away steeply there, some twenty or thirty feet down on each side, and one could look out over the tops of the brooding trees to a wide sweep of sky and sun.

I had just reached that embankment when it happened. There was the sudden roar of aircraft and that momentary stop-action glimpse of the snout of a P-51 as it erupted over the trees to my left. I did not wait to see if he was going to open fire; I assumed he would. I fled, terror-stricken, down the embankment to the right and into the trees.

I was not alone. The entire road was cleared instantly. Both the guards and the guarded dived for cover in the woods. Some made it only to the edge of the road and others were deep into the trees, but we all had one thing in mind; to find a hole and hide.

But he did not fire his guns. Having made the pass he climbed lazily into the clear air and came once again over our heads, but this time at several hundred feet altitude. He wiggled his wings as if chuckling over the joke he had played on us and then headed back to the west and home.

Slowly and painfully we came out of the woods and ditches and back onto the road. There were sprains and bruises and lacerations, but no one was seriously hurt by the encounter. We sorted out the packs we had dropped, bound up our wounds, and hobbled on toward the next stop.

When the war was ended and the world was trying to settle again into what passes for normal, I had business in a small town in West Texas. My car needed some repairs and I took it to the local garage and went about my own affairs. When I returned to pick it up I entered the shop through a side door and started across the floor toward the office when I saw that the mechanic was still working on it. And, as he worked he talked to a couple of idlers who sat on the workbench among the cast-off generators and spark plugs.

"And I said to myself: Now wouldn't they like to see an American airplane up close?' So I buzzed 'em. I dropped it down on the treetops and I come a'rippin' across that road with my cameras going. Musta scared the hell out of 'em 'cause they sure scattered!"

The urge to throttle a total stranger can be a powerful emotion. But I resisted. I took my car as soon as it was repaired and left town.

* * *

Somewhere in the back country of Bavaria there was a road that led up a long hill from the wooded, rolling countryside to a flat plain. In the American west it would be called a mesa, but I don't know what the

Europeans call such topographic formations. The road slanted gently up the side of the escarpment, following its contours as it rose at an easy climbing angle. The slope was thickly forested so that most of the road lay in shadow, giving it a penetrating coolness that brought out our coats again and made us step more briskly to ward off the chill. Back in the darkness of the woods there were patches of snow still clinging in the shadows.

Down in the valley where we had followed the stream for some two or three kilometers it had seemed like springtime. The sun had been warm and the smell of green growing things had permeated the air. But here, along this north-facing slope, we were plunged again into winter and our mood shifted to suit it. In the valley we had been cheerful and noisy, heckling the guards by singing parodies of popular songs, parodies in terrible German accents. But here we fell silent, intent only on getting to the top of the hill and back into the sunshine.

There was in that woods a peculiar smell, peculiar in the sense that it is common to such woods. It is compounded of the smell of pine trees, of rotting linden leaves and pine needles, of melting snow, and of fungus. It is not the vibrant, pungent smell of new growing things, of spring and new leaves. It is not even the earthy smell of mushrooms. It is a smell of decayed wood where no wood is in evidence, of rot and mold where only black pines and leafless lindens stand, a smell of death in the soft humus of the forest floor. The pine forests of Silesia and Poland have that smell as do some of our woods in North America. To me that smell still brings a somberness of spirit, an edginess that speaks of cold and hunger and prisons.

But we were not long on that hillside. The change in elevation was perhaps a hundred feet, the distance that the road wound up the slope perhaps half a kilometer. The change at the top was sudden and dramatic. The land leveled off and the forest stopped as if sheared off by some gigantic knife. Before us stretched a great expanse of level, freshly turned field where birds followed the planter, picking worms from the furrow. The sun glinted on the sweating backs of the horses while a wren sounded his territorial call from the hedge along the roadside.

The feldwebel called a halt there, to give us time to eat our scanty lunch. But I think he also wanted to enjoy the smell of fresh earth and spring after the walk up that hill.

We sat on the shoulder of the road, my "combine" and I, parceled out the cold boiled potatoes and meat pâté. I watched the farmer out of curiosity and perhaps from a certain sense of affinity for him. I had spent a good many days working with just such equipment and horses myself. He kept his head down, concentrating on his work. If he so much as glanced in our direction I was not able to detect it.

He went endlessly back and forth across the field, slowly working closer and closer to the point where he would have to turn his horses within a few feet of us. He came to that point as the *feldwebel* called for us to return to the road to continue our march. As we slowly reassembled our packs, as our guards hustled back and forth shouting "*Raus*!," he brought his team about and stopped them for a moment's rest. Then he looked up and his eyes swept the faces along the now forming column.

"God bless you, and good luck," he said in perfect English, then slapped the reins against his horses and went back to his planting.

* * *

We came again to the river, having descended from the high country in easy stages, staying overnight in a hamlet along the edge of the escarpment. We came to it at mid-morning and slaked our thirst with its cold clear water. It was deeper here and flowed silently between its grassy banks. It moved swiftly, swirling an early mayfly round and round before a fish rose to take it.

The roadway followed the river. The trees that arched over both were beginning to put on new leaves here, in this soft valley, and birds chattered and quarreled over territory in preparation for nesting. We passed through a village where women hung from upper windows and gossiped among themselves while their children ran along the streets, keeping pace with us and shouting questions to us. The admonitions of our guards fell on deaf ears as they tried to cram all their questions into the short time it took us to pass through the little town.

In the early afternoon we made our camp for the night. There was still time for us to go many more kilometers before it would be dark, but the plans had been made for us to stay in the barns of this village and we did not argue. The way we looked at it, the slower we moved the sooner we would be freed.

The village was larger than most in that area. Its houses were mostly rowhouses, like a teutonic version of a Welsh mining town. They straggled along both sides of the river in an irregular line and were interconnected here and there by arched stone bridges. What seemed to be a brewery straddled the river at the far end of town.

As we set up our Kriegie Kamp Stoves and began the task of assembling the bits and pieces of the evening meal we eyed the river speculatively. What would happen if we should jump in for a bath? Would the guards object? Or would the people who continued to go to and fro along the streets on either side be offended and ask that we be removed? We each thought these things but held our peace until Oscar spoke.

"Let's take a bath." He stripped off boots and socks in one movement and had his shirt half off before any of the rest of us realized that he really intended to go into that river to take a bath.

We could not let him do it alone. One man doing some unsanctioned act was too much a target for bullying by the goons. And besides, we were all dirty from the days on the road and our clothing had not been washed in weeks or months. This was a chance to rid ourselves of our filth and any lingering vermin that might have stayed with us from the camp at Nuremburg. In a matter of seconds half a dozen men were scrambling to find unbartered soap and to see who could get into the water first.

We ignored the disapproving stares of the passersby. We scrubbed our clothing, sending little swirls of soapsuds downstream, and laid them out on the grass to dry in the warm sun. Then we plunged back into the cold water and, like farm boys in a mill pond, made squirt guns of our hands and fought mock battles with the spray.

It couldn't last. Someone obviously had complained to the *hauptman* and he sent the *feldwebel* down to the water's edge to tell us that we must not swim here. Especially we must not swim nude. There were women and children who had to walk along the streets above us and it was not suitable that they should see nude men bathing.

We ignored him. It was not that we were being brave. We knew that nothing really serious was going to happen to us now because it was too obvious to everyone that Germany had lost the war and it was only a matter of time before we would be calling the tune. So we continued our water fight.

He reasoned with us until his reasoning changed to pleading, but we still stayed in the water with only our modesty and our wetness to cover us. In one last attempt at compromise he begged us, please, to wear our underwear. "Svim if you vill," he said. "But, please, vear *die unterkleidung*."

"Only when you bring them to us," Bob told him, and squirted water in his general direction. The *feldwebel* turned on his heel and marched, straight as a ramrod, up the embankment and out of our sight.

When our bodies were so chilled from the cold water that our teeth chattered, we put on our still damp clothing and went back to the business of supper. And the feldwebel never mentioned the subject again.

* * *

Somewhere in our ramblings about Bavaria we came to a village called Plankstettin. My notebook says it is a village and I must believe that it is, although my memories of it do not include more than a single dwelling with its attendant outbuildings. There must have been others, but I do not remember them.

It was in Plankstettin that Bob and I tried our luck with pigeon eggs. We were quartered that night in a cavernous barn where the rustling and cooing of pigeons made a constant gentle background to the noise of men setting out their blankets in the hay and starting cooking fires in the barnyard. As we ate our bread and cheese and sipped the thin coffee, we discussed the possibility that we might be able to gather eggs from the nests that lined the nooks and crannies of the rafters of the barn. If pigeon squabs were good to eat, then why not their eggs?

When our meager meal was finished and our blankets arranged for the night we made a survey of the interior of the barn. We looked especially for any high piles of hay or stacks of barrels which would allow us to climb into the rafters and so get at the nests. We were in luck, for in one dark corner of the great hay mow we found a ladder of sorts nailed to the wall of the barn and leading up to the cross-beam of the gable end. It was a narrow beam and offered scant footing, but it was a path into the tangle of cross-beams that laced back and forth beneath the ridgepole.

Bob went first along the cross-beam and pulled himself into the rafters, sending a flurry of pigeons swirling about that end of the barn. When the noise subsided and the pigeons sat on new perches eyeing us suspiciously, I followed him along the narrow walkway.

There was not room for us both in the rafters, not where the nests were, down at the low end where the roof met the cross-braces. So Bob crawled out as far as he could, reaching his hands into nests that he could not see into, while I hung precariously suspended by one hand on a rafter and my feet on the beam. Braced this way at a forty-five degree angle, I used my free hand to take the eggs as he passed them to me and to stow them in the pockets of my jacket. We must have collected three dozen eggs this way before we exhausted the nests that were within our reach.

We came back to the barnyard flushed with triumph and confident of a good breakfast the next morning. After all, it was still very early in the spring and the birds would have just begun to build nests and lay eggs. They would be nice fresh eggs and we would have them hot — fried, if Oscar could manage enough grease to fry them. But they would be good boiled, too. We were not really concerned with their preparation so much as we were proud of having produced such a store of good food for the men who remained in our "combine."

Oscar couldn't fry the eggs next morning not only because he didn't have the grease, he didn't have any kind of pan in which to fry them. The best he could do was to put them in a Klim can and boil them.

I think he must have had a feeling that all was not going to be perfect with these eggs because he prepared extra food that morning. Maybe it was just his sense of the rightness of the thing, that unexpected riches deserved to be enjoyed, or maybe he expected a disaster. Be that as it may, there was more than the usual toast and coffee laid out for us that morning.

Jake, the constant joker, was the first to crack an egg.

"Feathers!" he said. "This thing's got feathers!" And it did. One by one we cracked all the eggs only to find that the birds had been very near to hatching in all of them. And as we cracked them we dropped them back into the Klim can to be thrown away later. Those pigeons must have been very early starters at the business of nesting.

And, in the meantime, Oscar was down by the barnyard wall. We thought at first that he was just getting away for a few moments to himself, but then we saw that he was vomiting.

* * *

The *hauptman* had intended us to stay in the town of *Neider Ummelsdorf* that night. It was small enough that he would have no trouble guarding us and yet large enough to offer barns to house us all. From his point of view it had everything in its favor. He was a humane man and he preferred to see us at least under cover at night for, though the days had turned balmy the nights were still chilly. And there was a threat of rain in the air.

But *Neider Ummelsdorf* was not our kind of town. As he rode into the central square he realized that plans had to change and quickly, for the streets were patrolled by self-appointed guards from an SS unit. He didn't try to requisition barns for our use. He hurried back to the head of the struggling column with orders to go around the town and to continue to march. Then he drove on again to find another place for us.

What he found was *Holzlaiten*. Its four farmhouses with their attendant barns and sheds crowned the brow of a small hill, while all around them spread the fields on which they depended. It looked like something lifted direct from the Middle Ages. Only the Manor House was missing, otherwise it could have been one of those woodcut illustrations from a history book.

It was not an ideal arrangement. We were too many for so small a village. Most of us would have to sleep in the open farmyards, for the barns would not hold us all and the farmers voiced their displeasure at having us so near their cows and poultry. How did they know we wouldn't steal their milk and eggs, even their chickens if a chance arose? And the truth was that we would, for we had become master thieves, every man jack of us.

And that brings me to the point of the story. It was thievery that I had on my mind as I edged around the corner of the farmhouse, trying to look innocent and, at the same time, trying not to be seen at all. If I could just find out where the farmer kept his eggs maybe I could steal enough to liven up tonight's supper. Oscar was getting the fire going at just that moment, ready to cook anything we might bring in so that it could be eaten before the rightful owner would discover its loss.

Ordinarily we would have slipped out through the line of goons to go trading with the isolated farmers in the area, but tonight we couldn't risk it. We were still too near the goon squads of *Neider Ummelsdorf* to chance being caught. While the hauptman was inclined to turn a blind eye to some of our deals, his compatriots of the SS Troops would not likely feel so kindly. To be caught black-marketeering could mean a rather unpleasant death. And the *hauptman* would be helpless to prevent it.

So we stayed within the ring of pacing guards, not even taunting them to make them think we were going to slip away. They understood as well as we that this was no time for foolishness.

But anything within the village was fair game. So I sauntered along beside the building, hands deep in my pockets, head down as if deep in thought. Though I tried to be inconspicuous about it my eyes were searching each doorway and window of the barns across the yard, trying to discern which was the milk kitchen, for I was convinced that the farmer would keep his eggs there. In the two or three farms I had seen in Silesia it was in the milk kitchen that the farmer stored his eggs, cheese, and root vegetables as well as milk, so I reasoned that the farmers of Bavaria would do likewise. All I had to do was find the right door, slip in, fill my pockets, and slip out again. If I didn't get caught at it.

I was so intent on the barns that I missed the cellar door completely. Until I tripped over it and almost fell, that is. It was one of those sloping doors that project out from the foundations of old houses with basements, a sort of half lean-to that opens up and out to give access to a basement stair. And it stood open. That is to say, one half of it was open — I had stumbled over the other half where it lay closed almost at ground level.

This called for a change of plans. Furtively, I looked around to see if anyone had seen me. No one seemed to have noticed. I listened intently for sounds from the cellar below, but could hear nothing. I moved across the yard and waited to see if someone was down there after all and would come up the stairs at any moment.

I waited and waited, but no one came out. I moved again to the door and listened for the telltale sounds of people at work in the cellar. There was nothing. The smell of damp air spiced with sauerkraut came up strongly, but there was no sound.

I checked again to see if I were being watched, then ducked down the steps as quickly as I could. But I pulled up sharply as I reached the landing, for I didn't want to run helter-skelter into the midst of some situation I could not control. Or at least back away from if need be.

I peeked cautiously around the corner of the landing, not knowing what to expect, for a dim light glowed somewhere in the cellar and the air was redolent with the smells of food. What I saw was a vast larder stocked with more food than I had dared to dream of in months. Bins along the walls held turnips, potatoes, kohlrabi, even a few late cabbages that had not yet gone bad. At the far end of the room stoneware bowls held eggs in great heaps and hams and bacon hung from hooks in the ceiling beams. Crocks of pickles and sauerkraut rested in neat rows and beer barrels filled most of one wall. A light bulb glowed feebly on a drop cord in the middle of the room, but there was no one there.

I stood a moment sizing up the place, deciding what I would take. There was simply no way that I could walk across that yard out there with a ham or a side of bacon without giving myself away. Much as I would like to have them, the hams and bacon would have to stay where they were. And the sausages too. They hung in great looping chains along one beam, but I had no way to cut one loose nor to hide it if I did.

The eggs, yes. I could put those in my coat pockets with hardly a bulge and, if I walked very carefully, they would not break. But they were at the far end of the room next to the stair that obviously led to the kitchen. I turned my attention instead to the potatoes. They were nearer. They would not break in my pockets. I would take as many as I could conceal and get out before someone caught me.

"*Was ist los*?"

I jumped in fright at the sound of his voice. I had been certain that there was no one in the cellar, yet there he stood beneath the light, his hands on his hips and a little smile under the luxuriant mustache.

"*Was ist los*? *Stiehlst du kartofel anstatt fleisch*?"

What is this? You steal potatoes instead of meat? He seemed genuinely amused by this bit of peculiar logic. And he did not seem angry that it was his potatoes that I had been stealing.

I waited silently for the inevitable torrent of verbal abuse and the call for a guard. But he only repeated the question.

"*Stiehlst du kartofel anstatt fleisch*? *Warum*?" Why? Why, indeed! How does one explain the sort of logic that leads to such decisions? How do you say to a man, "I am taking your potatoes because I thought it less risky than taking your ham. I weighed the pros and cons and decided that I could not hide the ham, nor the sausage, nor any of the other things I would like to steal. But I could hide the potatoes in mypockets and no one would ever know." How do you say this to a man who has just caught you red-handed in his cellar? You don't. You smile wanly and shrug your shoulders and you begin to pull the potatoes out of your pockets and to put them back into the bin.

But he was not angry. He did not call for a guard. He did not berate me for stealing from him. He wanted someone to talk to and I was his captive audience. And he wanted to know why I chose potatoes.

When at last I had satisfied his curiosity on that point he moved on to other things. And as he talked he moved about the room doing the little tasks of a farm larder. He candled eggs expertly, shifting them from bowl to bowl as he did. He tested the state of fermentation of crock after crock of sauerkraut, sampling each and handing me a taste of it too. And all the time he kept up a running commentary on the state of the world in general and his own corner in particular. I wanted desperately to leave, but I could not without raising a hue and cry that would alert the guards.

And he tested the beer too. Without asking if I wanted it he took down two steins from the hooks and filled them to the brim with foaming beer, then handed one to me and set the other on the nearest kraut crock within easy reach of his right hand. He dragged a stool forward with his foot and motioned with his head for me to take another. And all the time he talked. He paused only long enough to push back his moustache and take long draughts of the cool and frothy beer.

He talked of the problems of farming when the weather was so unpredictable. Did we have such unpredictable weather in the United States too? But no, no one else had quite such foul weather as Bavaria. It would be too much to think that anyone else would have to suffer so. And he spoke of wartime restrictions on what he could make and sell. He seemed particularly irate at the limit on the strength of beer. After a second stein of it I was beginning to reel a little on my stool, but he seemed to feel that it wasn't nearly strong enough. Cat's milk, he called it.

On and on he talked, pausing now and again to draw more beer or to replenish the plate of sauerkraut he had set on the cover of a crock. Once he was interrupted by a call from up the kitchen stairs, but he made short work of that.

"*Nein, Mama. Spater. Spater.*" His booming voice carried a note of exasperation, as if he had been interrupted in some weighty business matter. And immediately he returned to the topic of the moment.

I don't remember what the topic was for I was getting more than a little fuzzy-brained by this time. All that beer — he never let a stein get empty before refilling it, to keep it alive, he said — all that beer was taking its toll. I was having trouble forming my words to answer his questions and I kept slipping back into English without realizing it. Each time he would good-naturedly insist that I speak German.

"*Nein! Nein! Ich bin Bayerish. Sprechen Zie Deutsch, bitte.*"

No. No. I'm Bavarian. Speak German, please. His voice, for all its booming heartiness, carried the sibilance of the Bavarian country speech. And his innate humor kept slipping through. Once he changed the "*Sprechen Zie Deutsch*" to "*Sprechen Zie Kraut*" and then laughed uproariously at his own joke. He had pronounced the "*Kraut*" with the particularly guttural sound of the North Germans and seemed to feel that this was appropriate to my situation at the moment. It was a gentle mocking of my own accented German.

The time finally came when Mama's mutterings upstairs could no longer be ignored. He rose, stretched himself with a great show of muscled arms and bulging belly, and shouted something up the stairs, something I didn't understand. Then he turned to me and spoke more slowly.

"I told her I would come up as soon as we had relieved ourselves. Come, I show you the way. Then you can go back to your friends with my potatoes in your pocket." He chuckled as he said it, still amused over my logic in choosing the concealable over the delectable.

Together we went out of the cellar, he going ahead to be sure the coast was clear, being sure that I would not be stopped by a passing goon and lose my few potatoes. He led me out along the barn to a stone wall very near the line of pacing guards. There we relieved ourselves of the burden of the beer, he with great sighs and grunts of satisfaction and I with a sense of thankfulness for the steadying effect of the relief and the fresh air.

I made my way unsteadily back to the packed earth courtyard where the others were already sleeping. I rolled myself in my blanket and fell instantly asleep. But I must have awakened someone for the next morning I found myself facing a barrage of questions, all of which pointed to the central issue of how does a prisoner of war, in enemy territory and under constant guard, get drunk!

* * *

On a mid-April afternoon we made our camp in an apple orchard. The village barns were too small to hold us all, and the weather was balmy. We spread our blankets under the trees and slept with the delicious scent of apple blossoms all around us. Our guards, too, seemed to be under the spell of springtime, for they turned a blind eye to our trafficking with the civilians who were eager for our cigarettes and soap.

The sounds of cannon fire, the rumble of tanks, the distant flashes of explosions, all the evidences of warfare which had been a constant accompaniment to our journey up to now, were absent that night. The countryside was as quiet and peaceful as if the war did not exist. We slept well, untroubled and content as only the young can be under such circumstances.

We awoke to a fairyland of diamonds and pearls. Dew drops and apple petals gleamed in the early sunlight like gems in the grass. We dawdled over breakfast, reluctant to leave this enchanted place.

Someone somewhere in the group, carefully screened by others so the guards would not see, set up his clandestine radio and tuned to BBC. He did that every morning. He carefully listened so he would be able to repeat the news to the rest of us. The Germans must have known we had some kind of radio but they had been unsuccessful in finding it.

Suddenly he turned the radio off, put it away in his pack. His face was stricken, white with anguish, and his hands shook. He did not run. That would have been a dead give-away, but he hurried to the senior officer. President Roosevelt had been reported dead. There could be no doubt about it. The information had come from BBC, not the German radio. The president was dead.

Most of us could hardly remember any other president. He had been our leader for twelve years. And now he was gone.

George, who was senior officer of that group, called immediately for a meeting of us all. He did not wait for confirmation from the *hauptman* nor the *feldwebel*. He told the guards we would not move until we had met. And we did not move.

We stood in solemn ranks among the apple blossoms while George and the Padre jointly conducted a memorial service. We were too stunned by the news to do more than react to what was said. And our reaction was an all-encompassing quiet. We stood in sparkling sunlight, the scent of the blossoms all around, subdued, silent, uncertain of the future.

And then we marched out once again on our road to nowhere.

But the smell of apple blossoms still brings back the memories.

VIII

Moosburg

In terms of acreage it was vast. In terms of facilities it was not. For the entire compound containing some six to eight thousand men there was only one latrine. The water supply was a single spigot in the middle of the area and the cookhouse was located in another compound entirely. Baths and laundry were just out of the question.

And across the fences in three directions there were other compounds containing other prisoners. There were British and Americans to the west, British colonials to the north, and to the east, behind double-guarded fences, there were Russians. The total camp had been built to handle less than a fifth of the numbers now crowded into it, so most of us lived in tents pitched hastily in the mud, improperly trenched and poorly staked. It would have been a truly miserable existence but for the fact that the distant rumble of warfare was a constant reminder that our side was winning the war.

The Germans made no attempt to keep us segregated by nationality or by compound. We were still required to stand the twice daily appell call in our own compounds — the gates between compounds were locked before the *hauptman* began his head-counting rounds — but for most of the time we were permitted to mingle at will. The British and Americans had always felt that certain kinship that encouraged mixing the two nationalities in the camps, but now we had others among us. There were the turbanned Hindus of colonial India, and Moslems as well. There were Africans and Arabs. And there were the Russians.

They came into our compound and walked about, their double-guarded status maintained only within their own area. They looked at everything with a great show of interest. And they asked questions about everything. But they were unwilling to enter into the bartering that had become a way of life in the camps. Our primary source of food was Red Cross parcels that contained both pork and beef among the canned items. The Hindus and Moslems brought their forbidden meats to us, the British and Americans, to trade for foods that were not forbidden by their religions. But the Russians would have nothing to do with any of this. They would not trade. Not for themselves nor for the sake of those whose religions demanded it.

* * *

We had time on our hands, and that is a dangerous thing for a group of Americans. If the war had not so obviously been ending in our favor, I'm sure the Germans would have had a hard time coping with us. But, instead of directing our energies toward escapes and harassment, we concentrated on the latest news of the front. Any bit of information, no matter how unimportant or fragmentary it might be, would be passed by word of mouth through the entire camp in an amazingly short time. And usually without too much distorting, too.

And other things, not related to the war and our coming liberation got passed about too. One day someone discovered that there was a small area in the Russian compound which contained women prisoners. This bit of news swept through the compounds like a Kansas prairie fire, setting off an immediate movement of men in the general direction of the women. They were impelled more by curiosity than anything else for, after all, there was the matter of fences and armed guards, which kept the sexes apart. But they went, nevertheless, to stand and stare, mute at the sight of women enduring the same hardships that we did.

I did not go to join the others in looking at the women. Somehow I felt it was indelicate, that I would be intruding on their privacy by my stares. But, on the day that we were at last freed, I saw some of those women in the *vorlager*. It was no wonder that the Germans had treated them with a grudging sort of respect. They could have gone bear hunting with a switch!

And we speculated on anything and everything: how far away the fighting was, when the liberation would actually come about, and if the goons would put up a fight to hold the town and the camp.

That last thought was of considerable concern to us because our available air raid trenches were in a sorry state of repair, having had their shoring timbers ripped out for firewood long ago. And, at very best, they would not protect more than half the men in the compound.

* * *

But we thought of lighter things as well. One of them was the classic question of what a Scotsman wears under his kilts. The question came up first, I suppose, in jest, but soon reached such an argumentative state that an authoritative answer simply had to be supplied.

And we had a source for such an answer. Jock, whose name was really Angus, had been taken at Dunkirk and had spent the intervening years plotting escapes and digging tunnels in first one camp and then another. And somewhere along the way he had acquired a kilt and a bagpipe. I don't know where he got them; perhaps it was what he was wearing when he was captured. Or he may have got them through one of the infrequent parcel shipments that the Germans allowed. Whatever the source, he had them and he used them.

The kilt served in lieu of pants, as kilts were meant to do. But the rest of his clothing had nothing in common with his heritage. In place of the Highlander's bonnet, he wore a British Army service cap jauntily tipped over one eye. Either his regimental coat had been lost or he never had one, for he wore a torn American battle jacket instead, its sleeves ripped out at the shoulders. And on his feet were the biggest combat boots I have ever seen. Jock was a big man, but those boots were gargantuan. Even on his big frame they looked ridiculous.

And he practiced on his pipes. Now the sound of a bagpipe can be a stirring thing when heard on the open moor or on the parade ground, but, in close confinement, it can be almost painful. But Jock was oblivious to all that. Every morning he took the pipes and spent an hour in practice. If the weather was good he would sit in the sun on the lee side of the only solid building in the area, the latrine. And that was not too bad, for he was out in the open air and the skirl of the pipes could dissipate itself. But, when the weather was bad, it was another situation. Bagpipes played in a tent could drive a man mad! Most of us would abandon the dryness of the tent for the comparative peace of the open, although wet, outdoors.

As I said, Jock could supply an authoritative answer to our question. Who, better than a Scotsman, would know what a Scotsman wears under his kilt? But we were a little reluctant to ask, for we were afraid that he would take it the wrong way and, when his anger was aroused, Jock could be formidable. So we argued about who should ask him, and, in the end, we drew straws to determine it. We might have dropped the whole thing except that some had placed bets on the outcome, bets payable in post-liberation currency.

As luck would have it, the short straw fell to the Padre. We thought this was great. First, it took the burden off our own shoulders. And second, Jock would never strike the chaplain even if the question made him angry.

Like schoolboys, we trooped along when the Padre went out to find Jock and his pipes. Finding him wasn't hard to do, of course; you just followed the sound to where he sat in the sunshine, his back against the bricks of the latrine and his arm pumping in and out as he fingered the notes of some obscure military aire. He eyed us suspiciously as we came to stand around him in a semicircle, but he didn't stop his playing until he had run the whole thing through twice. Then he lifted his hands to let the drone of the pipes die away.

"We hope you won't take it amiss, Jock," the Padre said, hoping to put him at ease before the circle of waiting faces, "but we've made some bets on it and we think you're the man to settle it for us. You being Scots and all that. What I mean is . . . the question has come up as to what a Scotsman - that is, what anyone . . .." He didn't finish the sentence, for Jock suddenly burst out laughing.

"Fine beggars ye be, the lot of ye!" He glared accusingly at us all, but the corners of his eyes still held the last traces of his laughter. "Puttin' the Padre up to doin' your dirty work! For shame!" And he laughed again. As his laughter subsided, bubbling and chuckling deep down inside, he stood up, towering over the Padre and seeming to be twice life-size with his torn jacket showing the breadth of his massive shoulders, the grotesque boots anchoring him firmly to the ground.

"If ye mus' know what a Scotsman wears oonder 'is kilts, I'll tell ye this: if 'e's a Kriegie 'tis naught! Past that ye'll 'ave to find oot of ye'r oon!" And he scooped up his pipes and marched away.

He had answered the question, but, somehow, we felt that all bets were off anyway.

* * *

I was a kid when the war began and, like most kids, I didn't think a great deal about the morality of war. My country was at war, fighting to save the world from the ravages that had already swept parts of Europe and were spilling over into the rest; fighting for our honor against an enemy who attacked without warning in a barbarous form of total war; fighting against the dictators of the world on two fronts simultaneously and giving a good account of herself on both. So, of course, I didn't question the morality of war. Like millions of others I volunteered.

And when I volunteered no one said to me, "So now you become a killer." No one spoke of the unpleasant truth that armies are intended for killing. There was that unspoken agreement to think of it as being something like the duty of a policeman; one does one's duty when one has to, but killing is a last resort when all other measures fail and it is kill or be killed.

A nation maintains an army for national protection, it is true, just as a city maintains a police force. But the similarity is very tenuous at best. A policeman's first thought is to save lives. A soldier's first thought is to save his own.

I don't mean to imply that soldiering makes a man a coward, for it certainly doesn't. But all of the training is geared to make him kill the enemy before the enemy can kill him. It is an impersonal sort of thing. That is not a human in your sights, but an enemy. He is not man, but monster. And, after a time, to kill a man becomes a way of survival.

Aerial warfare is a most impersonal sort of war. One sits in the glass-enclosed nose of a bomber, tracking little, black insect-like planes, firing one's guns when they come in close enough. But all sense of person-to-person contact is lost. It is just one machine against another. And the dropping of bombs is even more impersonal, for the only contact with the target is the moving map in the telescope of the sight. The reality of people on that map simply does not exist for the man looking through the scope.

Sometimes we spoke of the fact that ours was not a pleasant sort of occupation. Robby and I particularly used to get into deep discussions now and then of the less attractive side of our lives. But we always skirted around the fact that death was our business. Like all the rest of the American public, we were shocked when a flight crew named its plane "Murder, Inc.." This was being too blatant about a very touchy subject. We did not like to admit - we refused to admit - that, in their crude way, they were being honest.

And, in those first hours of my captivity, I think that I could have killed as dispassionately, as coldly, as anyone. For I didn't think of my captor as my fellow human, but as my enemy. As we rode through the alternate light and shade of the country road into Burg, I plotted his death as unfeelingly as if he had been some wild animal who threatened my safety. Not once did the thought occur to me: "This is a human being I am planning to kill." But, as I have said earlier, my chance never came to use the knife he so obligingly wore on his belt.

As time wore on I came to know so many of our guards in little ways.. Not that I knew many of them in the sense that I would consider them my friends. But I recognized the sound of the feldwebel's step even when I could not see him, and a certain ferret made a sniffling sound as he worked his way around under the building. If he intended his progress to be a secret, he failed miserably, for we could follow him from start to finish. The little human traits came out so that I was no longer able to think of them just as the "Enemy."

And then there were what we called the "trained goons." These were guards who, either for the love of their own creature comforts or from a genuine desire to see Hitler defeated, could be persuaded to supply us with some of the essential parts and materials for the building of shortwave radios, work permits for escape attempts, and information on a wide variety of subjects.

They risked their own lives in dealing with us in this way, and so we came to develop a sense of camaraderie that was no less genuine for its being cautious.

And in the process they became human. To us, I mean. They no longer were just the enemy, they were the human enemy. Most of us still were reluctant to admit that we no longer had the ability to be dispassionate when it came to death, but down inside we knew that we could no longer see life and death in quite the clear-cut way that we had in the past.

And so it came as a dreadful shock on that last day to see the building blow up. The word had been passed to us in great secrecy that some of the guards were going to stay behind when the main German forces pulled out. They were, for the most part, the men who had been our trained goons, but also included were some who simply couldn't see any other way out of a war that had gone sour with a vengeance. They had agreed to meet in a certain building as the pull-out began, and to stay there until they could give themselves up to the advancing forces of Patton's army.

The Americans and the *Luftwaffe* had agreed under flag of truce to exchange control of the town and prison camp without a fight. But the SS Troops changed all that. They saw the guards going singly and in twos and threes into the barracks building. They did not ask why. They waited for the trickle of men to stop and then they threw hand grenades in.

And then they manned their positions and prepared to fight.

To kill a man - even when that man is your brother. War was no longer impersonal.

The first tanks crossed the river in the mists of the very early morning. All night we had heard the clank and clatter of German armor as it was being pulled back in the continuing retreat into the mountain fastnesses of southern Germany. All night we had been shaken by the booming voice of the field guns newly installed in the woods beyond the fences. And all night we had lain, silent but wakeful, waiting for the silence that would mean that the city had been surrendered and, for us, the war was over.

But there were those forces about who were opposed to surrender in any form. There were those who would kill their own kind rather than see the city and the camp fall without a fight.

There were not many points in the camp where one could get a clear view of the town, but one of those places happened to be the little knoll just in front of the latrine. From that spot one could look down the service street of the compound, over the *vorlager* roofs and the intervening woods, and see the skyline of the city of Moosburg. It was dominated by what I took to be a church steeple, but which was, in fact, an architectural embellishment on the city hall.

As I stood there in the still chilly morning air, watching and listening as the American armor moved closer and closer to the town, and thus to me, I was acutely aware that the fighting had not stopped as we had expected. The field pieces still boomed in the woods, their muzzles lowered now so that the projectiles were screaming directly over our heads, and the rattle of small arms could be heard now and then amid the deeper sounds of the tanks. And from the tower on the skyline there was an occasional flash as a sniper fired down on the advancing troops.

I watched in fascination as the evidence of fighting moved through the city. By the smoke and dust and flying debris, I could gauge the progress of the battle. I felt somehow detached from it all even though I stood in fact in no-man's-land between the two main forces. I was a spectator witnessing the inevitable march of history. The thought that I might be in danger did not occur to me.

A rifle cracked in the woods behind me and there was the plaintive 'ping' of the bullet as it sang past me in the general direction of the town. Too late I realized that the air raid trenches were already crammed to overflowing and that there was no place left to find protection from the battle that was about to break around us. The goons were putting up a stiff fight to cover the withdrawal of their big guns.

I dived for the relative safety of the latrine only to find that it was filled with humanity and men were beginning to stack up against the wall, trying to stay on the American side, hoping to gain some measure of protection from the fact that they could be seen and recognized as POWs. As the fighting circled around the perimeter we moved with it.

And as we moved we could still see the tower on the building in town. The little puffs of white smoke, the tiny flashes of light continued to show themselves now and then, testifying to the fact that at least one goon had not given up the fight for the town. Long after the major push of the battle had shifted past us, those puffs of smoke continued sporadically.

But the end was inevitable. I suppose there were attempts to flush the sniper out by using standard infantry techniques but, if so, they were unsuccessful. So a tank was pulled back from the now rapidly receding front line. It was maneuvered into position along the main boulevard and there, at point-blank range, it blasted the tower out from under the sniper.

And from the doubtful safety of our brick latrine wall we watched as the Stars and Stripes were raised over the ruined skeleton of that tower. For us the war was over.

GLOSSARY

Ack-ack	Anti-aircraft guns or the projectiles fired by them.
Alles innen:	German words meaning "Everybody outside."
Appell	German word for roll call or head count.

AWOL — Absent without leave.

Bahnhof — German word for railway station.

Barracks — The plural form is used in a singular context by the military.

Bastille — Originally used to refer to the Bastille in Paris, it is also used to describe any prison, especially one for maximum security prisoners.

Bavaria — A southern province of Germany, centering roughly around Nurnburg and Munich.

Block — Barracks. A wood-frame building of one story designed as a dormitory. Internal arrangements varied from open-bay type to multiple rooms arranged along a corridor.

Blouse — The coat of the army uniform is always referred to as a blouse. An overcoat is called a coat.

BOQ — Bachelor Officers' Quarters.

Breslau — A town on the Oder River in the province of Silesia in the German Third

	Reich. It is now called Wroclaw, and is in Poland.
Burg	A small town north of Magdeburg, Germany.
Chemnitz	Once called Karl-Marx-Stadt. It is an industrial city in Germany.
Combine	Originally it meant all of those who lived in the same room in the block. Eventually it came to mean those who pooled their rations and shared the work of housekeeping and cooking.
Compound	A fenced enclosure within the total prison camp.
Comptez, s'il vous plaît	Count, please (in French).
Concertina Wire	Rolls of barbed wire between the two fences that surrounded each compound. It made escapes through the fences almost impossible.
Cook House	The central building of the compound. In addition to the central kitchen, where the German-supplied rations were prepared and distributed, it contained the offices of the Senior

Allied Officer, the Chaplain, some German officials, and the library. It was also known as the "soup kitchen" and the "cook shack."

Cooler	Solitary confinement cells.
D-bar	The chocolate bar included in Type D army rations. It was also included in most of the American Red Cross food parcels supplied to the prison camps.
Dead reckoning	A system of navigation that uses compass heading, wind speed, wind direction, and the speed of the aircraft through the surrounding air to determine the true speed and direction in relation to the ground.
Dead-stick	Landing without power from the engines; landing an airplane as if it were a glider.
Drogue	The small pilot chute, spring-loaded so that it springs out when the ripcord is pulled, which pulls the main parachute canopy out

of its pack.

Dulag Luft — *Luftwaffe* interrogation center at Oberurzel near Frankfort am Mainz.

Ein, zwei, drei — In German, the numbers one, two, three.

Ersatz — The German word means "substitute," but was used to de scribe anything that was non-genuine.

Escape Committee — A secret committee of ranking officers who were responsible for evaluating all individual escape plans for their practicality and their possible effects on others.

Committee approval was required before any escape plan could be supported by groups such as the Food Distribution Committee, Information and Communication, or the individuals who specialized in such things as forging German work permits or tailoring civilian clothing from overcoat linings and blankets.

Feather — To bring the edge of the propeller into the line of least resistance to the flow of air over it, so that it does not continue to turn and act as a brake.

Fécamp — The French town along the Channel Coast around which the American Army built its tent cities for returning prisoners of war and casualties of the front lines.

They were held there until transportation to the States was available.

Feldwebel — German for "sergeant." To us the term referred specifically to the sergeant who was administrative aide to the German *Kommandant*, the Commander of the prison camp.

Ferret — A German soldier who specialized in uncovering escape attempts by the prisoners.

Fire Pool — A concreted surface tank used to store water for use in case of fire.

Flak — Anti-aircraft fire; the bits of shrapnel sent out by the explosion of an anti-aircraft shell. The word had its origin in the German acronym for *fliegerabwehrkanonen* — flyer defense cannons — but was quickly incorporated into the English language.

Food parcel — The International Red Cross undertook to supply food to military prisoners during World War II. Most of the food we received came from the American Red Cross, but sometimes food packages from other nations were substituted. English, Canadian, Australian, and even Belgian and French food parcels were supplied on occasion. A careful record was maintained of what had been distributed so that no one would be getting less than someone else. All parcels were opened by the Germans before they were given to us and each can of food was punched with two holes so that it could not be hoarded and used for escapes. The holes permitted spoilage to set in relatively soon, even if we sealed the holes again with margarine as we did. But sometimes the German workmen would miss a can, either by accident or by design. When that happened the can was immediately exchanged for one which had been punched and the unpunched can became a part of the food stocks maintained secretly by the Escape Committee. Of course, the German authorities had no knowledge of this stock of contraband food. It didn't occur to me at the time, but I have often wondered since who it was who lived on short rations in order to provide those cans of food for exchange.

Fortress — The B-17 bomber; the Flying Fortress.

Frags — Fragmentation bombs; bombs designed to explode into thousands of fragments, depending on the shrapnel effect for their damage rather than on concussion.

Gestapo — The German secret police.

Goon — A German soldier. Also sometimes used to refer to any German, whether in uniform or not. A tame goon was one who could be bribed.

Goon tower — Also called goon box. These were observation towers placed strategically around the compound fence. Each one contained a machine gun mount that allowed the gun to cover at least 180 degrees as its field of fire.

Hauptman — The German word for "captain."

Hasenfalle — Rabbit trap.

Hausfrau — The German word for "housewife."

Hitler Jugend — Translates as "Hitler Youth." It was an organization devoted to preparing young people to serve the state. It was a sort of Boy-Scouts-Gone-Mad organization.

Honey bucket — A chamber pot, of sorts, which was kept inside the entrance to the buildings at *Stalag* XIII-D. It was necessary because the buildings were locked from sunset to sunrise and they contained no latrines. While we could have gone in and out through the windows, which were not locked, to do so was to risk being shot by the guards or mauled by one of the fierce dogs that were set loose in the compound each night. (During air-raids the guards withdrew the dogs and unlocked the doors so that we could use our air-raid trenches.)

Honey wagon — A wooden tank mounted on a horse-drawn wagon and used to remove the sewage from the latrines. The unprocessed sewage was used by German farmers to fertilize their crops.

Jerry — The Germans.

Jug — Nickname for the P-47 airplane, also called the

Thunderbolt.

Kein Eintritt	A German expression meaning "no entrance."
Kinder	The German word for "children."
Klim can	Klim was a brand of dehydrated milk. A generous can of it was included in each American Red Cross food parcel. Because it was the biggest can we had available, it was also the most often used in making pots, pans, and stoves.
Kriegie	Short for *Kriegsgefangenen* (prisoners of war). It was used by both the prisoners and by the Germans as a sort of slang term to describe any prisoner.
Kriegie Kamp Stove	Any of the portable contraptions we contrived and used for cooking our meals. They were usually made from flattened tin cans and ranged all the way from simple fire pots to elaborate, bellows-driven forges. Their greatest virtues were portability and the ca-

	pability to cook a meal with a minimum of fuel.
Kriegsgefangenen	German for "prisoners of war."
Kriegsgefangenenlager	German for "prisoner of war camp."
Lederhosen	Leather breeches.
Library	A small stock of books supplied through the Swedish YMCA.
Lightning	P-38 aircraft.
Lorry	British term for "truck."
Luftstutzpunkt	German for "air force station."
Luftwaffe	The German air force.
Magnesium bomb	Called bombs, they were actually small magnesium flares that were used in case of emergency to destroy the bombsight and the Mickey set to prevent their falling into the hands of the enemy. They worked by the simple means of burning anything they touched.
Mickey set	An electronic navigational aid, which was classified

as top secret during World War II.

Milk run	A slang term used to describe any bombing mission which had no opposition from either anti-aircraft guns or fighter planes.
Moosburg	A town in Bavaria, the site of Stalag VII-A.
Morderisch Amerikanisher	Translates as "American Murderer." Like *terrorflieger*, the term was used in a derogatory way to refer to American fliers.
Muskau	Bad Muskau, a town on the Neisse River in east Germany. It is now directly on the Polish border, but during World War II was well inside the borders of Germany.
Nein	The German word for "no."
Nicht rauchen	A German expression meaning "no smoking."
Nicht sitzen	A German expression meaning "no sitting."
Nord Deutch	(*Norddeutch*. In German it is written as one word.) North German. The

accents within Germany are highly distinctive. The differences between the speech of Silesia and Bavaria are like the differences between Bostonian and Atlantan.

Nuremburg — Bavarian city where *Stalag* XIII-D was located.

Oberstleutnant — The rank of Lieutenant Colonel in the German army.

Orderlies — Enlisted men assigned to work as personal aides to officers. In the European context they were essentially personal servants.

Pâté — A potted-meat supplied as part of the Red Cross parcel.

Perimeter rail — A wooden barrier placed 18 inches or so high and about twenty feet inside the perimeter fence. It served as a warning to keep us from getting too near the fence. It also served to mark an automatic home run in baseball games. Since we were not permitted to step over the rail without specific permission—in fact, were likely to be shot if we did—any ball that was knocked across the perimeter rail was considered a home run and the game came to a halt until we could get the attention of a guard and secure permission to retrieve the ball.

Polizeiwache — The German word for "police station."

Raus — Translates as "get out." It was the standard command used to get everyone outside the buildings for a headcount or for a search while we were in the camp. And it was also used to order us back into the formation while we were on the road.

Reich — The word means realm. It was used by the Germans to mean their government.

Safetied — Bombs were equipped with fuses that set them off according to a preplanned scheme--either on impact, after impact, etc.. To prevent premature explosion in the aircraft, each bomb fuse was equipped with a safety wire, which prevented an explosion before the bomb was dropped.

Sagan — The nearest town to *Stalag Luft* III prison camp. It is now Zagan, Poland.

SAO - Senior Allied Officer — The highest ranking prisoner in the compound. Although himself a prisoner, he could and did exercise a great deal of authority over the lives of the rest of us. Under the terms of the Geneva Convention and standard military tradition, the captor must permitthe captives to exercise the prerogatives of rank within the limits of their being prisoners.

Shroud — The lines connecting the parachute canopy to the harness.

Silesia — A geographical area formerly part of the German Third *Reich* and now divided between Poland and Germany.

Spãter — The German word meaning later.

SS — The Storm Troops of the German man army.

T-11 — A training aircraft used for training bombardiers.

Terrorfliegers — The German word translates literally as "terror flyers." It was used in a derogatory way to refer to Allied airmen.

Thunderbolt — P-47 aircraft, also called Jug.

Tracer fire — Incendiary rounds fired from a gun. Because the guns on aircraft were manually-sighted and fired it was necessary to provide some means of reference so that the gunner could know that his ammunition was going where he aimed it. This was done by placing an incendiary round at intervals in the linked belt of ammunition.

Trip-wire — The warning barrier inside the fence. In Stalag III it was a wooden rail and was usually called a perimeter rail. In Nuremburg and Moosburg it was a wire strung 18 inches high and about ten feet inside the fence. It served the same purpose in all three locations; it kept us from getting near enough to the fence to attempt any sudden escapes.

Une, deux, trois — In French, the numbers one, two, three.

Vorlager — Translates as "front camp." It was the administrative compoundthrough which all access to the other compounds was made.

Was ist los? — The German term means, literally, "What is loose?", but is used idiomatically to mean "What is happening?" or "What is going on?"

Wash — That arm of the North Sea that lies north of the English town of King's Lynn.

Wehrmacht — The German army.

Wirklich — The German word for "real."

Zuider Zee — The shallow body of water that the Dutch had partially drained to form additional farm land. When the Nazis invaded, the Dutch opened the dikes and flooded the land so that it again became a large, but shallow, saltwater bay.